"Lindy Ryan weaponizes the dread of grief suffered
in isolation. Horrific and heartbreaking."

JAMIE FLANAGAN, screenwriter, *The Haunting of Bly
Manor, The Fall of the House of Usher*


"*Cold Snap* is an intrusive thought, an open wound.
It will consume you."

STEPHANIE M. WYTOVICH, Bram Stoker
Award®-winning author of *Brothel*


"*Cold Snap* reads like a whiteout of blinding grief.
The deeper you plunge into this haunting novella,
the more you lose sight of your surroundings. Before
long, you won't be able to tell where the pages end
and reality begins. It's that immersive."

CLAY MCLEOD CHAPMAN, author of
*What Kind of Mother* and *Ghost Eaters*


"A powerfully affecting study of bereavement,
illuminated by a sense of the uncanny and mysterious
that builds to vivid scenes of breathless nightmare terror."

RAMSEY CAMPBELL, World Fantasy Award-winning author


"Steals through your soul like a winter chill—a heart-
rending, darkly humorous hymn to grief, guilt and
love. This is a perfect Christmas horror story that's so
crisp and cool, it'll leave your fingers frostbitten."

JOSH WINNING, author of *Heads Will Roll*

# COLD SNAP

# LINDY RYAN

**TITAN** BOOKS

Cold Snap
Hardback edition ISBN: 9781835410080
E-book edition ISBN: 9781835410097

Published by Titan Books
A division of Titan Publishing Group Ltd
144 Southwark Street, London SE1 0UP
www.titanbooks.com

First edition: October 2024
10 9 8 7 6 5 4 3 2 1

A CIP catalogue record for this title is available
from the British Library.

Printed and bound by
CPI Group (UK) Ltd, Croydon, CR0 4YY.

"A sad tale's best for winter: I have one of sprites and goblins."

—Shakespeare's *The Winter's Tale*

# 1

The Toyota's trunk slams shut.

The sound reverberates up the length of Christine's spine, shudders against each vertebra, crawls under her scarf. It forces a puff of breath from her that freezes her hands to the steering wheel. She peels them free, furling and unfurling gloveless fingers to get the blood moving before she presses the button to start the engine, then cranks the defroster. The speakers crackle with static. Even in her own driveway, she can't get a signal. Her thumb taps on the steering wheel to turn the volume down, and she pulls her scarf tight around her throat.

Twin chartreuse ovals glare at her from inside the open pet carrier in the co-pilot seat, but Christine knows better than to try and coax the cat out. The family pet, like her son, always favored Derek.

The rear passenger door jerks open, hinges screaming in the early morning quiet. Frigid December air floods the interior—she hadn't thought the SUV had warmed up at all, but it's even more frigid outside. The little hairs at the base of Christine's skull shiver to attention as the Toyota rocks with the weight that jostles into the back seat.

Cold rips the air from her lungs when the rear door slams shut. Tiny crystals paint the air before her face, and she jams her chin down into her scarf. A flash of yellow catches her eye, as the wind outside whips the ribbon strung between the four sawhorses that block the concrete steps to the basement.

Another shiver races down Christine's spine and she cranks the heat as far as it can go. "They design the doors and trunk to close without slamming, Billy." Her snide tone slices through her lips before she can think better of it. "No one here to impress."

The cat glares at Christine from the carrier. She could have said something nice to her son. Something patient. Something *motherly*. To offer something other than a thoughtless reminder that it's just the three of them now—her and Billy and Haiku. No husband, no father, no favorite human. Her words hang heavy between them.

The angry crinkle of his parka swallows Billy's grunt as he shrugs into his seat, the hiss of his sleeve reaching for the seat belt. He pulls the belt across his chest and the polyester growls. The buckle bites down hard as he slides in the metal latch. One knee pokes between the front seats. She cannot believe the length of her son's legs in his torn jeans.

Christine closes her eyes. There's a *snap*, and—

Derek's foot slips. His features go wide, one eyebrow arching high enough you'd think it would touch the hook-shaped scar that's marked his forehead since he was six. The whites of his eyes grow bright, brighter, blinding. Christine lunges for her husband's hand. Grips nothing but air.

Fur brushes the back of her fingers. Christine's hand flies up from her cold thigh and she jumps in her seat before her eyes snap open. The cat recoils onto the co-pilot seat but doesn't retreat into the carrier. The chartreuse eyes are unsurprised, maybe just embarrassed for her. Billy scowls and looks away from the mirror. Buttoned up to his chin, the parka doesn't turn with him. Christine lifts the carrier, and the messenger bag she'd put between the cage and the seatback almost falls on the cat. She wedges the carrier in the footwell and leans her bag against the seat to make room for Hai. As she closes her eyes again, her fingertips trace the feline's back.

Haiku rolls under her touch and Christine presses her palm into the soft ginger. The cat's purr rumbles, and she counts the short spaces of quiet between each heartbeat.

Milliseconds.

That's all it was.

One thousandth of a second between the time when Derek was there, with her, on the roof of their two-story suburban home, and when he wasn't.

"Chris—" He'd only had time to say half her name. The last time she would ever hear it.

She had not seen him hit, saw only the empty space where he'd knelt that millisecond before. Christine heard her husband's spine snap. The rush of breath as life left his lungs.

Then Derek was gone.

Gone days now, probably. She doesn't know how many. Still, she wants to say that it feels like longer. A month, maybe. A year. Time moves different when your world stops turning.

"But he's not gone." Christine's eyes flicker open, and she looks in the mirror, but Billy didn't say anything. "Derek's right here," the voice says.

The crackled fog ices the outside of her driver's side window, but she can make out the red rectangle of her front door, framed by gray sconces. No figure stands at the door. Derek should be checking the locks, peeking in through the window to make sure they'd left no lights on. Her light. The table lamp at her end of the couch that she never remembers to turn off.

A dark blot marks the bottom of the door. "See," says the voice. "His boots."

A pair of wet-weather stompers stand on the front porch mat, tall and black and caked with snow. Derek must have set them there to dry went he went inside the house. Any second now and he'll burst through the front door, head to the car, slide in the co-pilot seat beside her. Christine strokes Haiku's shoulders and gets ready to take hold and get the cat back into the carrier.

She blinks and looks back to the porch. Billy left his own dark green boots there, they're not Derek's black pair. She meant to throw them in the trunk.

She blinks again. That goddamned lamp burns through the window, from the end of the couch. And her husband is dead. He's gone and their son shuffles around in the back seat, wondering why the hell she isn't getting a move on.

"Sorry," she whispers. *Sorry this happened*, she wants to say. *Sorry you're in pain. Sorry he's gone.*

"I'm sorry I snapped." Christine clears her throat and speaks to the steering wheel. "The noise startled me. That's all." She tugs the scarf up over the bottom of her chin.

*I'm sorry it was your dad that died, instead of me.*

In the back seat, Billy clears his throat, trying to make the sound take up the whole interior of the Toyota. The chill seeps back through Christine's fingers and she bristles. Once, she'd fuss at him for acting like that. Once, it would hurt her feelings. But she deserves her son's derision now, doesn't she? After all, she had wanted to put the Christmas lights up before Thanksgiving instead of waiting. It was Christine who'd insisted she help Derek string bulbs around the eaves instead of Billy this time. Christine who reached for Derek's hand and caught air instead.

"Your fault."

Christine's breath fogs the air in front of her face, wraps around her brain.

She meets Billy's gaze by accident in the rearview.

"Your fault," the voice, not Billy, says.

Her lips form another apology, but Billy's phone chimes first. His eyes tear away, ripping the knife free of Christine's body. He thumbs open his phone, works his fingers over the screen. She looks away from the mirror when he reaches for the metal buttons on his parka. She grits her teeth when he *snap, snap, snaps* them open.

Derek's foot slips…

Christine clenches both fists until her skin threatens to break under her nails. "You got everything?" she asks.

Billy snorts.

"Toothbrush, face wash?" The way her voice rises, she sounds like the kid. "Underwear?"

"*Mom.*" The word comes out half-exhale, half-growl. "Face wash? I know how to pack a bag."

She bites her lips into a line and nods. Of course he does. Her son is fifteen, not five.

The layer of ice across the bottom of the windshield cracks, then slides away in streaks that turn the house liquid on the other side of the glass. Snow blankets the roof, and there's no one to turn the Christmas lights on, but Christine can make out the empty spaces where Derek hadn't finished stringing them up. Tears bank behind Christine's eyelids as she studies the strings that he did finish.

She holds the tears there. Lets them sting.

The twin sconces spark on at either side of the front door, followed by a row of sharp white incisors that bite into the frost hanging over the rain gutters. Christine gasps and Haiku vaults into the back seat. The messenger bag falls onto the seat again, and Christine flips it against the seatback too hard.

She's surprised that the lights could have scared the cat as much as they did her—but it must have been the way Christine herself jumped that sent the cat flying.

Three red bulbs for every five whites. Derek had wanted the pattern to suggest holly berries tucked among frost.

"I turned the timer on." Billy's dry words scratch at Christine's throat. "Dad always turned it on when we left home."

She blinks away dark spots the lights have burned in her vision.

"That a problem?" her son asks.

Christine can't stop blinking. "Why would it be?"

Billy's parka crinkles as his phone chimes again. "Whatever."

The tired muscles around Christine's mouth force her lips into a smile so tight her jaw aches. "It's not a problem," she says. She pulls the scarf loose around her neck.

The engine purrs and her eyes finally relax. Icy fingertips reach up and she finds the tears have wetted her eyelids, without creating the waterfall she'd imagined.

"I'm glad you remembered," she says.

She dries her eyes with the edge of her thumb, little movements so her son won't notice. She does not tell him that his father would be proud.

In the back seat, he grunts.

Christine sighs as she rummages in the pockets of her down jacket, extracts a square wad of paper. The listing for her destination used the word *scenic* twice, which she's come to understand means her navigation app will get her close, but no cigar. Derek had scribbled directions onto the back of an old envelope, and Christine has folded and unfolded the paper so many times the familiar strokes of his handwriting have all but faded. Is this the last piece of his handwriting? How much longer will his words last? How long before he disappears completely?

The yellow tape on the sawhorses catches her eye again, and she vows to replace the railing herself, once they get back.

Warm air blows in off the engine and Christine shifts the Toyota into reverse. Asphalt crunches as the small SUV inches down the driveway, backs out onto the street. She shifts, spins the wheel, and accelerates too fast. The hours—weeks?—since Derek's death have taught her not to look at the neighbors as she winds her way out of the cul-de-sac. Not looking reduces the chances someone will phone later, to say they'd seen her drive past, which was such a coincidence because they'd *just* been thinking about her.

Did she need anything? Whatever she said, they'd bring over a casserole.

Everything would get better after the holidays.

Christine grips the gearshift and keeps her gaze trained straight until she passes the last stop sign out of her subdivision, makes the left turn toward the turnpike, and falls in behind the monolithic back of a semitrailer.

In the rearview, Billy's attention doesn't leave his phone.

Christine follows the truck around the on-ramp to I-95. She pulls at the scarf so it lays across her shoulders.

"It's been a long time since we went up into the mountains," she says when the silence squeezes her lungs. "Remember that camping trip a couple of summers ago?"

He makes a sound that could go either way.

She pulls onto the interstate headed north and pushes the gas all the way down to get out from behind the semi.

"Right after you finished fifth grade." They took the trip to Allegheny as a treat before Billy started middle school. They'd been stationed in Ohio then. Billy had to remember, because they'd spent the whole weekend mispronouncing words just to make the National Forest's name rhyme.

*Billy-Goat finished ele-menny.*

*Now we're campin' in Allegheny.*

"Remember?" she asks.

Christine glances in the rearview. Her son's Adam's apple bobs, but his eyes never stray from his phone.

"Well, I hope you put that thing down for at least *some* of the drive," she says. "We could sing carols? Like when you were little? Do you remember any?"

*Billy-Goat finished ele-menny.*

A deeper grunt this time. More dangerous. The distance between them widens a bit more.

She bites her lip. The distance isn't new. But Derek had been the rock beneath their family, solid ground to Christine and Billy. Without him they float free, drifting like the fog outside the Toyota's windows as the sun inches higher into the sky.

Christine thumbs the steering wheel stereo buttons. She taps the volume until the low buzz becomes a hum, revealing a voice, then a song. She clicks through the pre-programmed stations, waits out a few notes before recognizing a classic rock song, then a holiday tune, and so on. When she makes it through the dial and Billy hasn't so much as twitched, she shuttles the radio back to NPR. British-accented voices drone on about Iranian music, and she lowers the volume until it's an indistinct murmur again.

"Well, get your fill of phone time now," she says. "You won't have service when we get into the mountains." Guilt oils her insides as she imagines the kid's boredom. "It'll be just you, me, Hai, and the trees. No phones. No emails. Nothing."

Billy's foot thumps against the back of the co-pilot seat and the messenger bag somersaults on top of Haiku's vacated carrier. "You brought your laptop," he says, full of righteous teenage judgment. He's caught her in the act of some wrongdoing. "So much for no work over the holidays."

Christine counts to three. "I did not bring my laptop," she says, and smiles into the mirror. "Just a couple of books." Her eyes flick to the chestnut swath of hair at the top of Billy's downturned head, the too-bright blue of his parka. The orange cat curled in his lap. "My phone is going off just like yours when we get there."

Nothing this time, not so much as a grunt.

Tires grind across miles of asphalt. For a while the highway is lined by town after city after town, but soon it opens up to farmland, then mountains loom ahead. Morning turns to afternoon. They near the mountains, but as the SUV climbs, they lose sight of any peaks. When you're in the mountains, you don't see mountains, you just see the earth rise and fall. Trees tower all around, and occasionally some distant peak appears, then hides again.

Christine's lips sting and her stomach rumbles. They should have stopped for coffee. The Toyota's key fob rattles around alone in the cup holder. Breakfast always improves Billy's mood.

The car shoots over another state line and Christine shifts in her seat, taps her fingers on the wheel. Billy still hasn't managed to peel himself away from his phone.

"Want to play a road-trip game?" she asks.

He snorts. Maybe there's a word in there, she doesn't know.

"I've got a couple of audiobooks," she offers, "if you want to listen? There's a new podcast—"

Grunt.

"Billy!" Christine doesn't mean to shriek. "Put the phone down for two seconds and *say* something." The rubber of the steering wheel is hard and cold as metal against her palms, and she veers too close to the cars as she passes them. "Give me a sentence. Just a sentence," she begs, staring too long, too hard, into the rearview mirror, at the stranger in the back seat wearing torn jeans and a bridge of peach fuzz across his upper lip. "Just *talk* to me."

The tires hum across asphalt wet with melted snow. The sound grows louder. She can almost hear a teapot boil over, and the air grows stiff in the car as tension swells between them. Snaps.

Derek's foot slips. His features go wide—

"You want a sentence?" The way Billy bites off the words sends Haiku scuttling across the back seat. "I'll give you a sentence. It is stupid that we are driving all the way to Pennsylvania to spend Christmas in some stupid cabin." He drops his phone on the seat, pulls the cat back into his lap, and chews at his lip. "Why are we still going?" He looks away. "We shouldn't even celebrate Christmas," he mumbles against the window.

"Christmas is about family." Christine pretends to pay attention to the road so she doesn't have to look at her son. "I don't think there's any better time to remember that."

"So we could at least spend it with Grandma and Grandpa," he says.

"We just saw them at the…" She can't bring herself to say it. The f-word to end all f-words.

Billy scrunches up his face. "My *other* grandparents, then."

"Papa is allergic to Haiku," she reminds him. Again.

"Could've left her at home." He says this looking down at the cat's back, scratching between her ears.

"She's family."

"Oh my god!" A chill blows in from the back seat. "She's a *cat*!" Billy says.

Christine almost says, *She's all we have left*, but says instead, "Haiku is family—and Christmas is about family.

We're honoring the holiday plans Dad made for our family and spending Christmas in the P.A. Wilds."

"Plans *Dad* made." Billy snatches up his phone, jabs at the screen with his index finger.

"That's right, Billy," she snaps at the mirror. "Your father loved the holidays, and he—"

"Is *dead*," Billy deadpans. "Dad's dead and you want to go on vacation." His foot thumps the back of the seat again and he turns his face to the window. Angry breath paints the glass white. He doesn't turn all the way, but just enough that she can still see the corner of his eye.

The sun can't reach the road, and the evergreens all around are black with shadow.

"Dad isn't here," he says.

"But we are," says Christine.

*We'll head up into the mountains*, Derek had said, all the way back to Halloween. *And have a good, old-fashioned Christmas*, he said as he held her on the couch, sick on candy that no trick-or-treaters had claimed. *Just the three of us*, he said, *and the trees*.

*Don't forget your cat*, Christine had said. *But won't it be lonely?* she'd asked. *Just the four of us? And the trees?*

Derek's mouth had spread in a jack-o'-lantern smile. *But that's the point*, he'd said. *To get away for a while.*

Away.

By late December, that had sounded better than ever. Away from well-wishers, casserole-bearing neighbors she'd never spoken to outside of tragedy. Away from that damn house, the railing she needed to replace around the basement door, her husband's ghost, and the Christmas lights he'd never gotten the chance to finish.

"Just the three of us," Christine whispers to herself, to the road, to the empty co-pilot seat beside her. "The three of us, and the trees."

# 2

In the building marked *Office*, a little handmade sign on the reception desk declares *No Pets!* Age and the tips of hundreds of ballpoint pens have carved wrinkles across the wooden surface of the desk. Now dust claims the grooves. Christine traces her fingertip across the ripples and spots a second *No Pets!* sign on the wall.

"Reservation is under Sinclaire," she tells the woman across the counter. She spells the name aloud, landing hard on the E.

After they'd decided to spend the holidays in the mountains, Derek had done all the research and reserved the cabin. He'd promised that he'd found lodgings as far away from anyone else as he could, in the name of privacy. The big woman frowning behind the desk had to be Armentia, who, as Derek had explained, must never know that they'd bring a cat.

Armentia pulls up the reservation on an old Mac that looks like the back of the tan Keurig Derek brought home two Christmases ago. "I've got a Derek Sinclaire," she says, making a sour-candy face. Her nasal voice drags the first syllable, so it sounds more like *Deer-rek*. She meets Christine's eye with a smirk, as if she's caught her in a lie. "You don't look like a Deerrek."

Christine fixes on the best smile she can. "Derek is my husband." She says the name evenly, without emphasis. Her tongue tastes like salt.

But she's said *is* again, hasn't she? Not *was*.

*Derek* was *my husband*.

*Deerrek was my husband*.

Armentia's lips pinch into a line so tight it looks like her face has cracked across the lower half. One eye opens bigger than the other. Bigger, and gray instead of green, the same shade as the woman's houndstooth pullover.

"Pardon?" Christine says.

Armentia is one of those tough old broads no one ever considered attractive, and she probably never cared. The pissed-off set of her face suggests she's also the kind of gal who wouldn't hesitate to kick a widow and her son out into the snow right before Christmas.

"I asked you," Armentia says, "if your husband will be checking in with you." Her mismatched gaze falls to the gold band wrapped around Christine's ring finger. "The reservation is under *Deerrek* Sinclaire, not Missus."

Armentia squints out the window at the SUV with Jersey plates. "Why didn't you both come in," she asks. "Why only one name on the reservation?" Christine parked next to a pickup truck with local plates, which she guesses belongs to Armentia. A faint puff of exhaust rises in the cold air behind the Toyota. Christine remembers shoving the cat carrier below the dashboard and hopes Billy has a hold of Haiku, though from here they can't see much through the windshield.

Phantom frostbite curls under her cuticles, flash freezes the metal on her finger.

"I mean, think about how it affects other people," Armentia says. "Why'd it even have to be one or the other of you?"

*Deerrek was my husband.*

Probably most couples put both names on their reservations, didn't they? Christine flinches, jams both hands into the pockets of her down jacket. She pretends to dig around for something.

"He's not—" She reaches into her pants pockets, to make extra good on the act. "Not joining us." She pulls out her wallet, and with a flick of her wrist, holds her driver's license and two credit cards over the counter. She tucks her wallet and the hand with her wedding band back into her coat pocket. "Just me and my son," she says. *No pets.*

"Your son?" Armentia says, staring out the window again.

"Billy." Christine pulls at her scarf, then holds the cards out again. Derek probably neglected to add a child onto the reservation, too. "He's fifteen."

Christine's hand floats over the reception desk. Armentia doesn't take the cards, just steeples her fingers together, elbows on the scarred countertop. She shakes her salt-and-pepper head. "You need to add everyone in your party onto the reservation," she says. "And if the name of the person checking in changes, you need to let us know beforehand. I can't go and give the cabin to anyone who has the same last name." Her voice goes up at the end like it's trying to form a question, dare her to disagree.

Christine stammers, and her hand droops with her smile. She picks the hand back up, flutters the cards in her fingers like lifeless white flags.

Like a website that finishes loading, the pattern on Armentia's fleece pullover comes into focus. Rather than traditional houndstooth, each little tilted shape reveals itself as a tiny cartoon terrier, ears at attention.

"I'm sorry," Christine says, unable to look away from Armentia's chest. "I didn't… I didn't realize."

*I'm sorry, my husband died and I didn't decide to come until yesterday.*

"Especially this time of year," Armentia says, as if Christine hasn't spoken. "Cabins book up months in advance. We have to be extra careful about who checks in and out." Armentia clacks at her keyboard as two sleeves' worth of alert scotty dogs glare across the counter.

"I understand," Christine says. Other than Armentia's Ford 150 and the Toyota, there are no other cars in the lot. A smooth layer of powder has either blown off the roof onto the windshields, or fresh snow has started to fall. Enough to keep more risk-averse vacationers off the mountain roads.

She straightens up, despite the weight of the cards dragging her hand down. She hopes her own coat isn't covered in cat hair, as the pack of tiny houndstooth terriers will surely snuff out if it is. The enthusiasm for the no-pet policy suggested by the signage surprises Christine, considering that fleece pullover.

"I should have called. I apologize for the hassle." Christine bites her lip. She almost asks if many people canceled but thinks it best to say something optimistic. Maybe Armentia is, like Christine's father, allergic to cats. "We're really looking forward to spending Christmas here, though."

*I'm sorry, my husband died and my son will never forgive me if I've dragged him all the way up here for nothing.*

Armentia looks at the cards but doesn't touch them. "Takes two minutes," she says, sucking her teeth, "and saves me the paperwork."

"I'm happy to pay an extra deposit," Christine says, "some kind of change fee, if that helps?"

*I'm sorry, I just buried my husband and if you send me back to that fucking house I will well and truly lose my shit.*

"Is an extra deposit going to do her paperwork?" the scotty dogs bark.

The cards tumble to the counter. Slip through the wrinkles in the wood surface. Lost in the void. But Christine blinks, and they lie fanned across the counter, white flags thrown down in surrender.

"I just thought—" she stammers, and tugs her wallet back out. She isn't against a bribe, not if it works. Not if it means they can stay.

But the folded leather explodes between clumsy fingers, scattering paper and plastic across the desk—cards she hasn't bothered to return to their slots, a few wadded-up bills, a rumpled stick of gum showing pink through the worn foil wrapper. A slip of newspaper. Ink blurs where tears have dimpled the paper, but his face is there. His smile. The little hook-shaped scar on his forehead.

Derek.

*Deerrek.*

Frost settles between Christine's shoulder blades. She shivers and reaches for the paper, but the hand that covers the obituary isn't hers, the fingers too thin, too pale. Too long, with too many knuckles.

Armentia's hands rest on her keyboard. Her eyes flick across the mess.

*Claws*, Christine thinks, but the hand moves and the fingers pinch the paper and it's Christine's own hand.

She shoves the clipping back into her wallet and bites her tongue to hold back her tears.

"I'm sorry," Christine says. She trembles and covers one hand with the other. "I should have called. I didn't think and…"

"All right, it's all right." Both of Armentia's eyes are green now. Her smile seems soft enough to be real. She holds a key ring in one hand, and with the other she picks up the gum and the cash and scattered cards and stacks them neatly. She picks up the two credit cards Christine had first spread across the counter, looks at her screen, and adds one of the cards to the pile. Her eyes go back and forth from the screen to the card that Derek must have used for the reservation, then hands the card back to Christine with a smile.

"There's no sense in getting all upset about it." Armentia dangles the metal keychain between them. "You sure you and your boy want to be so far out there, all by yourselves?" she asks. "Can get lonely."

Christine nods. *Just the three of us and the trees.* If she speaks, she'll scream.

Armentia's voice lowers into a whisper. "I've got a fancier suite close to the main lodge. Our deluxe cabin. Now, I like to hold onto it, in case of—" Christine doesn't catch what she mouths even though she leans in close enough that her coffee-breath clogs the air. "But it's yours if you want. No extra charge."

Christine exhales for the first time since saying, *Derek is my husband.*

Armentia will let them stay.

Christine shakes her head and does her best to smile. "Thank you," for the offer, for not turning her away, "but we'll be fine in, ah, in the one we reserved?" Christine plucks her things from the counter and stuffs them in the wallet, making no less of a mess than before.

Armentia's hands hold two keys now. The new one has a flimsy plastic fob, not a heavy metal ring. "Go on and take both," she says, "just in case you change your mind." Armentia drops the keys in Christine's frozen palm, then gathers a handful of colorful paper flyers and thrusts them over the counter like a stack of board game cash. "You're all the way down in Cabin Eight. No cable, but there's a DVD player and a few old discs. Wi-Fi, too—it's slow, so hope you're not in a hurry," she says. "You'll find the password on the kitchen counter, next to the coffee pot."

She tussles the flyers until Christine accepts them and says, "Thank you."

"I'm here in the office until seven," Armentia says. "Captain Pizza down the road stays open 'til nine. It's not great, but it'll do if you're not up to cooking." She flicks the corner of the papers in Christine's hand. "You got the menu."

*Shit.* Christine remembered clothes and presents. She packed Haiku's litterbox in the trunk, a Duraflame log, the Rockefeller Christmas puzzle they'd been putting off doing for three years, and every box of hot cocoa Derek had bought early and squirreled away. She's brought the pork shoulder, the pan, and all the trimmings for the Yuletide feast. But she hasn't thought to bring any actual groceries to sustain them to the holiday. Worse, Christine can't remember the last time she's eaten a decent meal or fed Billy something that didn't come out of a neighbor's casserole dish.

"Is there somewhere close I can pick up a few things?" she asks. "Get a cup of coffee?"

Armentia's lips purse, caught between another round of disapproval and newfound pity. She points at the giant map pinned to the lobby wall. "There's a mini-mart down the road if you're looking for a loaf of bread. You want more than that, you gotta drive about ten, eleven miles for a Wawa or a Giant Eagle," she says, and flicks the color pages again. "You got the addresses. But if you need to go, do it while you still can." She nods toward the window, where a thicker layer of white coats the gravel parking lot, the trees that line it, though the black slash of road beyond is clear for now. "Lots of places start shutting down early for the holidays," Armentia says. "Even the plows won't make it out this way if we get more than a few inches." The rise of her eyebrows suggests that they will.

Christine thinks of Stuart Ullman handing Jack Torrance the keys to the Overlook Hotel. The thought makes her smile and shiver at the same time. "Don't worry," she says, "I won't get lost in the hedge maze," she mutters.

Jack Nicholson's crazed, frozen face blinks at her. Derek's glassy, unseeing eyes replace Jack's. When Christine blinks again, her own icicle eyelashes and purple mouth peek back at her from a sea of white.

Armentia gives Christine a look like she might want to take her keys back. "Nothing like that up this way. Just two-point-one-million acres of wild forest from here to Allegheny and Dark Skies." The frown turns into a grin. "You know in the book they were topiary animals?"

This surprises Christine so much she can't speak, and Armentia misreads the expression. "The novel, *The Shining*?" Armentia says. "I love animals." Christine can't help but look to the multiple *No Pets!* signs. "My favorite one of his is *Cujo*." The kaleidoscopic terriers on the pullover nod in agreement. "Got our share of drunk fools now and then, but most all the critters hibernate this time of year. Except moose."

"Moose?" Christine hasn't considered wildlife.

"Blind as bats but meaner than hell. You or you boy get out to playing out in the snow and you see one, you run," she says, flaring her mismatched eyes. "They won't chase you very far and if you go into the trees, they can't maneuver their racks easy through the branches." Armentia crooks a

31

finger up on either side of her head, then nods at Christine, moving her antlers in sync. "Won't need to worry about freezing in any fancy landscaping if one of them catches you," she says. "They'll stomp you so far into the ground, I won't find your body 'til spring."

Christine goes cold.

*Just the three of us and the trees.*

Derek hangs twisted around the railing like a discarded coat, and there's red on the snow and all down the concrete steps to the basement.

Maybe Armentia remembers the soggy slip of newsprint with the blotted portrait. Or maybe Christine's face has lost its color, gone rigid, frosted over. Armentia has come in front of the counter, and the pissed-off set of this tough old broad's face has fallen and now she smiles too hard. But she pushes Christine toward the door, outside, waving goodbye. She mentions firewood and waves around the corner and says don't forget it gets dark half an hour earlier up in the mountains. Christine's boots crunch through white to the dirt of the parking lot. Billy stares at her, his face rigid behind the icy glass of his window, the most eye contact he's given her all day.

# 3

**B**illy doesn't talk as Christine parks the Toyota in front of Cabin Eight, its roof covered in a smooth coat, thick and white, unmarked by any footprints.

Billy hugs Haiku in both arms so that, even if someone watches, they won't make out her shape inside the puffiness of his parka as he silently carries her inside. He doesn't say a word as they unload their luggage, cover the sofa with the brown grocery bags, mostly filled with wrapped packages all labeled *From Santa* in Derek's handwriting. The cat shoots under an equally fluffy armchair that Christine wants to collapse into and—

Derek's foot slips...

Christine rubs her arms, presses the SUV's lock button on her key fob, and closes the cabin door against the frostbitten air. The few things still in the car can wait. Her stomach rumbles.

A watercolor landscape of mountains hangs above the mantel of a small, soot-rimmed fireplace. The artist went unusually dark for watercolors, but Christine's no expert. Notes of cedar and pitch permeate the air, the scents sharp and tangy over an undercurrent of someone's grandmother's stale perfume.

Christine flicks a switch in the kitchen and the light fixture buzzes over the three-seat dinette set. Three of the four bulbs burn white, but the fourth pops, turns black. Christine feels the snap in the back of her neck.

Derek's foot…

She tries to cover the sound in her brain, she starts to speak, but can't form a whole thought. Blown out. Her filament burnt. She zeroes in on the painting, the mismatched furniture, the tattered carpet in the main room. One might call the cabin quaint. Rustic.

Devoid of any holiday cheer.

Billy plunks himself down at the kitchen table. With the set of his shoulders her teenage son redefines the word *sulk*.

"We can spruce things up in here," Christine says. A rip the length of her forearm runs through the rug. A threadbare buffalo blenkty hangs over the back of the two-seater sofa like the black and white wool wants to hide something. She lets herself lean back beside the grocery bags and digs slippers out of Derek's duffel bag. Her feet slide out of her boots and into the sheepskin slippers with

34

the indoor-outdoor rubber soles—though she couldn't wear them out in this weather. "Make it festive," she says.

Her son's grunt upgrades to an eyeroll. She can't blame him.

She reaches over to pinch the wool cover, which doesn't smell too bad. "Hey, remember why you used to call this a blenkty?"

He exhales so long and slow he hums a little at the end.

*Billy-Goat finished ele-menny.*

When Derek suggested a holiday in the mountains, he sold Billy on promises of snowball fights and long winter evenings of chestnuts roasting on an indoor fire. Christine he'd seduced with visions of an idyllic Christmas cottage— garland-trimmed surfaces, stockings hung on a mantel, an evergreen shining in the corner.

The blurry watercolor study of mountains reminds her of Manet. Or Magritte? Black-as-night shapes under a pale sky.

Derek's Christmas cottage is not at all like he must have imagined. Not so much as a sprig of wilted mistletoe in the shadowy rafters overhead.

Christine wanders toward Billy, glancing around the room so it won't look like she's stalking him. She wracks her brain for a dumb joke to tie the funk of old-lady perfume to grannies who got run over by reindeers. Fat men in red, stuck in chimneys. On rooftops.

The words go flat in Christine's mouth. She sucks in a breath, pressing the heels of her slip-ons into the thin linoleum flooring.

They should have stayed home. Home with the railing to replace and the concrete stairs to try washing again, because that was terrible, but Derek's not here and that's worse.

Billy pushes out a lungful of air. He shakes his head at the corner of the room. Christine doesn't see anything to complain about, then guesses it's what he doesn't see there.

They didn't get a Christmas tree at home either.

Haiku growls from under the armchair, a low rumble that ends shrill. *Deerrek*, the sound seems to say, and it makes Christine blurt out, "Jesus, Hai!"

The cat's green eyes spark near the floorboards.

"What, Mom?" Billy says. "Someone has to say something."

"I've just never heard her do that before." Christine knows the deep growl did not sound like a name to her son, not anyone's name. She knows this.

"You've never heard our cat purr?" Billy asks.

"Okay." Christine clears her throat loud enough that she can't hear her husband's name anymore. "So it's not exactly what your dad had in mind." She puts her hands on her hips, looking from the entryway through the kitchen and into the den, if you can call it that. Chartreuse eyes stare back from under the fluffy chair. A narrow hall bends to the right, toward two bedrooms and a bath. "But there's a fireplace and I've got a bag of chestnuts." She jerks her thumb toward the stuff piled on the sofa. "We can work with this."

Billy raises an eyebrow. "You brought the cast iron?" He stands up. Did she pass too close?

She plays a quick game of fill-in-the-blanks and comes up with *skillet*.

To roast chestnuts, they'd need a skillet.

To hold over the flame.

The small kitchen belongs in a cheap motel. She'd be lucky if Armentia supplied an aluminum pan. Copper, maybe.

"Didn't think so." Billy lets himself fall onto the cushion beside the gifts and pulls his phone from his pocket. He taps the screen, lays his head on the backrest, and begins fiddling.

"No service," Christine says.

"*Minecraft* works offline," he says, eyes glued to his screen.

"That's not the point!" she snaps. "That's not why we're—" she says. "Why your dad wanted—"

Derek's foot slips…

Billy's face does not move as he slips the phone into the pocket of his parka, both hands disappearing inside as well. His quiet reaction stings, even though it shouldn't.

She's surprised he put the phone away, that she retains any authority whatsoever.

To stop her fingers from trembling she runs her hands over the kitchen's yellowed appliances and brittle utensils. An undersized refrigerator, an ancient toaster oven, a single-burner electric stove. Everything appears functional, she'd expect that much from Armentia. More than sufficient for lodgers who rely on frozen dinners rather than home cooking. The five-cup coffee maker looks suspect, but the orange light comes on when Christine pushes the button on its base.

A white laminated card propped up against the machine bears the promised internet password. On the kitchen counter, next to the coffee pot.

Christine stuffs the little card in her pocket with her wallet.

She remembers the lamp still on beside the couch back at home and thumbs the coffee pot off. In the freezer, a thick white crust pushes in from every direction toward the center, overwhelming the dull metal trays, the kind with the crank up along the center to force the cubes out. The trays are empty inside, but frost climbs the outsides from each direction. The top crystal layer crumbles to the touch, the glacier more solid underneath.

"What are you doing?" her son asks.

She pushes the freezer door closed. "Gotta run down to the grocery store," she says. She leafs through the colored pages she'd thrown on the dinette table. "Any requests for solstice dinner? Only comes once a year." She thumbs the address for the Giant Eagle into her phone, but the map can't connect. Maybe when she gets back to the road.

Billy snorts. "Twice." His bottom lip juts out as he gives the bags beside him a quick once over. He scowls at the black and white wool of the blenkty over the back of the sofa and takes a quick sniff.

"What?" she says, scrunching her face at him. "Solstice," she remembers. "Right." Summer. Two equinoxes, two solstices. Little bookends on the seasons.

Billy pushes himself to his feet and drops his phone face down on a narrow end table at the end of the sofa, then sidles to the kitchen without looking at his mother. She knows he watches from the corner of his eye. He yanks open the refrigerator door, exposes the empty shelves, swings the door shut.

"You didn't bring any normal dinner food," he says. He could at least sound surprised.

"The check-in lady up at the lodge gave me a flyer for a pizza place," Christine says. "How do you feel about half-cheese, half-veggie? Kind of fun symbolism for the solstice."

Her son's eyebrows pull together. "Huh?"

Christine rubs her palms, spreads them flat in front of her as if looking for a hug. "You know, like the Holly and the Oak Kings," she says. "Each solstice they fight.

In the summer, the Oak King reigns. Tonight, it's the Holly King's turn."

"What's that got to do with pizza?"

What *does* that have to do with pizza? "Balance?" she tries, but the answer sounds weak, even to her. "Two halves of the year?" Hands still in front of her, she mimes a circle, slices it down the center. "Of the pizza?"

"I'll make a sandwich." Billy squeezes past her and rummages through the grocery bags on the sofa until he finds one with food. He tucks a tin of cocoa and a shrink-wrapped pack of candy canes under his arm, studies a tub of crispy fried onion that Christine bought for the green bean casserole, then leans his head back and groans.

"You didn't even bring bread and stuff?" he says. "Cereal? Nothing?"

Should forgetting to bring the bare essentials destroy that last trace of parental authority? Further convince him that she isn't prepared to handle things as a single mom?

Billy's eyes bore into her. There's no sense in pretending.

"I had to bring the special items because I didn't know if I could get them here," Christine says, which is true enough. "So now I can grab a few things before we settle in. Help me make a quick list."

"Why didn't you just stop on the way up?" he asks.

The cold is so dense in the cabin that Christine's breath hangs in front of her when she sighs. She thinks about putting her coat and scarf back on and realizes she hasn't taken them off. "Didn't see a grocery store." Also not a lie. "Do you want to go with me?" she asks.

Billy grunts a no, and she notices that she can't see his breath. Maybe the room is not so frigid as she feels. When he snatches his phone up from the narrow end table, Christine pats the laminated card in her pocket and closes her eyes.

Armentia did not exaggerate. Christine pulls into the empty lot of the Giant Eagle just before nightfall to find all the windows black except for the neon beer ads. The hours printed on the door promise that it should be open another two hours, and from the warmth of her front seat, she spies no note about any early closure.

The dashboard clock reads five p.m. Plenty of time to get back to the cabin and phone for pizza—unless they shut down early too, or Billy's hunger has gotten the better of him and he's already ransacked the trimmings for the holiday feast. Not that it matters. Is a feast for two still a feast, or is it just overeating?

Christine's stomach turns at the thought of whatever greasy slab of wheat and tomato sauce you can get from Captain Pizza. Another meal delivered by a stranger, but at least a delivery driver won't ask how she's doing, if she's been getting any rest, taking care of herself, staring too long at the bathtub, the kitchen knives.

Christine always answers with a smile and a nod, because that's what the people asking want. They don't want to hear about how she doesn't sleep, rarely showers. How she keeps waiting to see her husband walk in the door, while she can't stop seeing him fall off the goddamn roof.

A light pulls her eye back to the Giant Eagle, but it's just a timed bulb flicking on above the gray, plywood bulletin board. Pines sway behind the market and to one side, and the sky drains of color back the way she came, even the trees. A thin layer of snow fades the gravel parking lot to a pale shade of concrete.

A few days before Christmas, less than an hour before nightfall, and Christine has to drive another ten to find a grocery store that isn't already locked up tight for the holiday.

By the time she makes it all the way back, the gray afternoon has deepened into evening—she tries to see the color in the evergreens, but they've faded to black. The dust blowing down from the sky has hardened into clumps. Temperatures in the teens drag into the single digits, likely to continue downward. It's hard to imagine the Oak King reclaiming this lifeless landscape.

As she pulls the car onto the snow-caked gravel and turns toward Cabin Eight, the check-in lobby is as dark as the Giant Eagle, the pickup with the local plates gone. Armentia had said she'd stay open a couple more hours, but despite her need to book out full for the holidays, if

42

anyone else has taken up residence in the other cabins, it doesn't show. Christine knows the deluxe cabin is empty, wherever that is.

No lights. For sure no campfires, or cars.

"Not a creature stirring," she says to herself, as the SUV creeps past Cabins Two and Three, into the forest.

Under the heavy silver dark, a patch of blue sky still shows through behind the white-covered treetops. The Toyota's tires crackle over frozen gravel and dirt. Between the gray and the dark and the quiet, all signs point to more snow—and a lot of it.

"Dreaming of a white Christmas," she sings softly. How wonderfully, perfectly, tragically idyllic. When his orders came through to relocate back to the Northeast, the first thing Derek talked about was a white Christmas morning. Snow had fallen on Thanksgiving, and a neighbor told them that sometimes it came as early as Halloween, once as late as Mother's Day, but winter weather was not as reliable as it used to be. Derek had kept his fingers crossed for Christmas. No matter where they lived, Derek wished for a white Christmas ever year, and now his wish had finally come true. He just hadn't lived to see it.

A holiday carol drifts through the speakers—"Baby, It's Cold Outside." Christine twists the knob, cutting off the not-so-happy couple. She ticks the windshield wipers faster and glides the wet sole of her boot back and forth across the gas pedal. Three more days. Just another seventy-two hours and Christmas will have come and gone, and she and Billy can get back to—

*To what?*

To an empty house. A home with a hole in it.

She presses the brake and the car crawls to a stop at the log rack. Someone, probably Armentia, has painted the words *Honor System* across the top of the plastic structure, which looks like a store-bought doghouse with the front hacked off. The little firewood stall leans against a larger wooden structure set into the ground. Framed plywood stands with a sheet of Plexiglas bolted onto it, covering a set of the colored flyers that Armentia gave her. One hooded light bulb pokes out of the top of the board, but the bulb is out.

Christine lets the engine and lights run and steps out to stuff a few arm-length chunks of firewood around the flimsy plastic bags in the trunk. A chill pricks through the thick puff of her coat. Ice forms in her eyes, her nostrils, and she pulls her scarf tight.

"...gone..."

Her head jerks up, but no one's there. No sound at all, other than the dull rumble of the car engine, the squeak of wiper blades. Maybe Armentia had just closed shop but lingered on the property.

Maybe Christine had heard the last of the voice.

But she did hear something.

"Not gone."

She drops the log but doesn't hear it hit the snow. If she makes it back to Cabin Eight and Billy asks her why she walked around the front of the car, she will not even remember having done that.

All around, undisturbed snow and dark, silent cabins. She can't see the lights of Cabin Eight past the hard bend in the road up ahead.

A shape moves just outside the beam of her headlights. The scarf itches at her throat and she tugs at it.

The figure stands in the thickening gray night, wrapped in frosted fog and shadow. Christine squints, as if she could will the houndstooth pattern of Armentia's pullover into focus. Tall and thin, the figure hangs in the hollow dark between trees. In a moment it could slip through the branches, be lost in the dim.

It doesn't move. Whoever it is, it's not Armentia. Arms hang like tree branches weighed under heavy snow, and when the figure shrugs, Christine hears snow crash down, though it seems to fall from above, from the branches around the figure's head. He barely moves, but with such care, so slow.

A black hole opens just above the huge shoulders, stretching wide at the top, and Christine's eyes snap shut, knowing this is the source of the voice, the voice she's heard since New Jersey.

The wind moans around her, a chorus of ghosts.

A breeze picks up. Snow pricks her cheeks, and Christine shields her eyes with her palm. She tries to call out, but the wind fills her mouth with frost.

The black hole in the face expands. If this man has a jaw, it's impossibly long.

"Christine," the figure calls.

Words freeze on Christine's tongue.

She has not heard anyone say her name more times in her life than she has heard Derek say it. Not even her parents. And although he had many ways to say it—from *What do you wanna watch tonight, Christine?* to the more serious *Could we have a conversation, Christine?* to the curt *WTF, Christine*, the *Don't let me fall off this fuckin' roof, Chris*—there were many variations, but each one was his.

And she recognizes that inflection. She knows her husband's voice, and the figure calling to her sounds like winter itself.

"You're not gone," the voice says.

Christine squints into the dark. Her eyes stiffen as tears frost over, they seem ready to burst from her face, and her fingers stretch out slick and sharp as icicles from her hands.

It's just the wind.

Just the wind, playing tricks.

*Just the three of us and the trees.*

The figure inches into the light. He grows bulkier with each tiny step, somehow darker as he comes out of the shadows of the trees, moonlight reflected in the branches that twist above his head.

As the figure steps onto the road, breaking the silence of the night with the crunch of a man's weight on powder, the loud crackle of ice breaking, the snap of—

Derek's foot slips…

"Christine."

The mouth stretches black and wide as a cavern to suck her in.

She wants to go to it, to him, to Derek, and her body slides across the snow that gathers in the narrow road, along the path of her car's headlights. Her feet make no sound, do not break the surface of the falling—

Snow dances down from overhead.

Christine blinks, and when her eyes open she stands alone at the edge of the woods.

# 4

Christine and Billy don't speak over dinner.

They never really do, not anymore, but this silence clouds the dinette table, chokes any flavor out of the greasy cardboard pizza. The corners of the pizza hang over the cutting board as another bulb flickers, goes dark, overhead. A shadow falls across her son's face, stealing his eyes from her. She hates the silence and she welcomes it, afraid of what she might say.

The man in the woods looked nothing like her husband. The way he said her name, though, that had reminded her of Derek. In that strange voice formed on rushing wind on falling snow in frozen air—

"Moose." The word cracks through her lips. Armentia warned Christine about the moose just like she'd warned about the snow, the closed stores—

Billy shoots her a look over the table. "Moose?" he says

around a lump of cheese. "What are you talking about?"

Christine takes a bite and chokes it down. She still hasn't taken her coat off. "Think I saw a moose earlier," she says, wishing she'd kept her beanie on, too. Her short hair curls around her face. Shadows hover at the edges of her vision. "When I got the firewood."

Billy looks at the bags on the green Formica countertop. "You got firewood?"

Her teenage outdoorsman is as unimpressed by moose as he is surprised that his mother stopped for wood.

She nods, takes a bite then feels too tired to chew it.

Billy seizes the last pizza slice from the cutting board and bites off a mouthful of congealed dairy. "Where is it?" he asks, and chews.

The disbelief in his voice prickles through the down of Christine's coat. "Trunk," she says. She doesn't mean to sound so cold when she adds, "Waiting for *someone* to help. Took me three trips to bring the groceries in." She wipes her fingers on one of the cheap napkins that came with the cheap pizza and swallows. "You could've at least helped me put things away."

Billy grunts. "You got it all before I could get my jacket."

He takes another bite of frozen pizza, and she suppresses her own eyeroll. When she'd gotten to the open grocery store, twenty miles away, she'd grabbed a pizza rather than bet on Captain Pizza staying open. No way would they deliver as the snow picked up. Only while the girl at the register sacked her groceries did Christine check her phone for signal and realize the better reason for the frozen pizza. If she waited to get back to Billy before calling in their order, she'd need to connect her phone to Cabin Eight's Wi-Fi, which would mess up her whole internet deception.

But *Minecraft* works offline.

Her son makes no move to follow her to the kitchen counter when Christine stands to clear away the finished meal. Worse things lurk outside in the winter air than a few plastic grocery sacks—things that howl your name and watch you in the dark. With fingers like sapling branches.

Billy's molars crush against crust, his tongue makes toilet sounds, repositioning the pizza in his mouth.

A squelch as his jaw works at the glob in his mouth.

A deep suck plunges it down his throat.

Snaps.

Derek's foot slips. A green line coils in the air before him. His features go wide, eyebrow arching... Such a familiar expression, almost comical if it weren't—

Christine spins, snatches the plates from the table, grimaces when a thumb slides across a spongy oil stain and the plate smashes to the floor like a man hitting an iron rail. It doesn't break. Billy stares at the pale blue plate, the color of a hospital dressing gown, his open mouth exposing a wad of bread, if you can call it that.

She grabs the pizza box off the electric stove top. Not a square, corrugated box, like Captain Pizza might have delivered, but the flimsy, damp box from the frozen aisle, which crushes so easily.

This is the last meal they will eat out of a box. The last bites of pity food that will ever go into her son's mouth.

Billy hangs his head and crosses his arms on the metal edge of the kitchen table.

This trip will be the last of a lot of things. She tosses the box in the trash can.

A few bits of cat food kick around the bowl Christine placed in the corner of the kitchen. She spots Haiku sitting on the back of the sofa, warm on top of the dingy wool cover. Apparently the black and white blenkty passed the kitty sniff test.

The only clue that her son has moved at all: the plate that didn't break on the floor now sits on the table.

She removes groceries from the bags, places them as though these cabinets were her own. Tiny puddles form on the plastic counter where items have sweated out their frost. Not knowing where to find a dishcloth, she wipes the wet away with the wrist of her jacket. This trip is the last time for take-out pity parties and sympathy casseroles. The last time for silent dinners, silent car rides. The last—

The front door creaks open. Slams shut.

"Billy." A package of pasta drops from Christine's hands to spill across the floor. The sound of Lego bricks dumped out across hardwood. The cat stalks down the hall away from the den and all the drama.

Christine presses her nose to the kitchen window, but can't see around to the front, only trees, the white-speckled sky.

She listens for crunching snow.

A car door slams and Christine's heart stops. She throws the front door open as thunder crashes against the porch slats. Billy wipes his hands on his pants, standing over a small pile of wood, and squints at her. Snow cakes his Vans, up around his ankles.

She looks at the logs. "Is that all there is?"

He screws up his face. "This is all you got?" He nudges one of the logs with the toe of his sneaker. "Can we even get a fire going with this?"

Christine stares into the dark over her son's shoulder, glares at the shadows until they take shape as snowy tree branches, and not the shovel-shaped antlers of a wild animal.

*Just the three of us and the trees.*

"Did you see the Duraflame in the trunk?" she asks.

Billy's teeth chatter. Snowflakes gather on his arms, but he stands defiant in shirt sleeves and torn jeans and frowns on the stoop beside her. The thin layer of frost forming on his shoes cracks when he shifts. "Did you bring some matches," he asks. "A lighter?"

"Camping kit in the trunk, next to the first-aid kit." Finally, something she *has* remembered, if only just because Derek never shut up about keeping them handy. Glacial air tickles against the hollow of her neck and Christine tugs at her coat's zipper, then crouches to pick up two of the logs. "Your boots are back there too," she says, and feels around her throat for her scarf. "Grab them so you'll have something to wear since you decided to freeze your sneakers."

Armentia's words come back. About moose stomping bodies so deep into snow they stay there 'til spring. Their hostess, who loves animals, and whose favorite Stephen King novel is *Cujo*...

Christine blinks it away.

Billy rolls his eyes, but he trudges back into the snow and pops open the SUV hatch. The bright yellow wrapper on the Duraflame log appears jaundiced in the silver moonlight. The boy slings the camping bag over his shoulder and stuffs the log under an arm. He leans into the trunk, but comes up empty-handed, staring into the dark space. "Seriously, Mom?"

The expression on her son's face is frostbite. She can't see what he sees, and she bites down rather than asks.

He reaches in and comes out with a black pair of stompers. "These are *Dad's* boots," Billy growls.

Tall snow-caked boots on her porch at home. The ones she'd thought proved Derek had come back, waiting on the other side of their front door.

Billy dangles the boots in the air before he tosses them back into the trunk.

*You'll be taller than me*, Derek had said, *by the time you're done.*

Billy stood against the doorframe of the master bedroom closet. Derek held the ruler firm over his head, swiped the charcoal pencil against the wood trim, like the marks that ran all the way to the carpet, ages and dates counting down. Christine recorded the date beside the pencil line and teased, *I sure hope so. Gotta fill out those hands and feet.*

Billy had looked away. Back before he'd watch her from the corner of his eye. She had hurt his feelings, had forgotten how sensitive he'd become. Emotional growth spurt, though you'd hope for the opposite effect. She'd been the same at that age—waterworks as regular as Old Faithful. A fragile type, her mother had said.

*As handsome as your Daddy, but bound to get taller*, Christine told him, and Billy's mouth had reworked itself into an almost-smile.

Derek had clamped a hand on Billy's shoulder, tugged him close. *Good*, Derek said, *someone can finally get stuff off the high shelves*, he said, and Billy's almost-smile bloomed, as the boy missed the look that his father had given his mother.

At fifteen, now Billy's feet are two sizes larger than Derek's.

Bigger feet and bigger hands, too.

"I'm sorry," Christine says. Billy's boots are green and Derek's are black. "I must have gotten them confused."

If her son grunts, the wind sucks it away.

Christine almost apologizes again but chews her lip instead. "Don't forget to double-click when you close the trunk," she says, one fist raised to mime proper use of the key fob. "Or the light stays on and kills the battery."

Billy slams the trunk shut, fumbles around in his back pocket with the fob before bumping against Christine's shoulder on his way into the cabin, timed right with the double beep of the Toyota's locks. She tries to say something as he disappears down the short hall, but the words pile up in her mouth and a door closes inside as Billy shuts himself back away.

Her breath dissolves in the air. She slides her hands into her pockets, shrinks inside her coat. As snow falls like ash from a charcoal gray sky, the winter night that Derek would have found so magical is strange and hostile around her. He'd sold her on the lure of getting out of cell range, away from inbox notifications, away from everything except—

*Just the three of us and the trees.*

As Christine stands outside the unfamiliar cabin, stares out at a landscape rendered in dark gray, pinned down by trees where things move unseen between branches, she wants to run. Leave the kid the keys and run, let the snow fly up from her footsteps and run past Armentia's dark lodge down the empty highway and run from all of it once and for all.

She kneels in front of the fireplace. They'd lived in a few houses with fireplaces, as she and Derek moved around the country. She's never seen a smaller one. Setting down two of the logs she got from the plastic doghouse, the ends stick out the front of the fireplace. She props the Duraflame on top and lights its corner with a long fireplace lighter from the camping bag. A low, steady flame with a blue center crawls across the wrapping, not enough to bring her skin back to life. Down the hallway, Billy goes from room to room, yelling at the cat. The wrapper burns all the way across the top of the Duraflame, but if Christine pictures it totally engulfed, she can't imagine how it'll catch the logs below it. So she pulls the wooden shafts out, dropping the self-start log onto the ashen concrete bottom of the fireplace, and sets the raw logs on top of it like a ramp. The wrapper stops burning where the ends of the wood logs rest on it, but the center of the Duraflame keeps going, and the wrapper burns away to the wad of recycled material inside.

Her giant of a son towers over the dinette table, arms out in a shrug, the closest she's ever come to hearing him say, *What the fuck?* in her presence, and she's pretty sure he's come close a lot of times.

"I'm sorry?" she says.

"You got AirPods in or something?" His pale legs show through the torn jeans, ankles peeking out from under the hem. When she snarls and points at her naked ear, he says, "I yelled for you."

She jerks up to her knees and shakes off the fog. "Sorry, I thought you were talking to Haiku."

"I can't find her."

Christine checks the back of the couch, where the cat had been perched on the blenkty…

Her son snorts, pounds his fists on his hips, and walks into the kitchen. He comes back holding the empty cat bowl. He sets it on the sofa, jerks that away from the wall, almost knocking over the end table and spilling a bag of gift-wrapped boxes across the floorboards.

"Whoa," she barks, "whoa!" and stomps her knees over to the presents. Billy reaches down for the bags, and when he picks that up, the rest of the gifts fall out. She yelps his name.

"What," he says, "not like you got me the Hope Diamond."

"Hope—?" She laughs. "Where did you even hear that. I don't think the Hope Diamond will break if you drop it, but know what would?"

He hands her the empty grocery bag and picks up a flat, rectangular package in bright red paper. "iPad Pro…?" Some of the gifts have tags *From Mom & Dad*, but she can't read this one as he shakes it.

"That? I think that's your *My Perfect Ponies* paint by numbers." The Duraflame roasts beneath and between the wood logs, and Christine tears the paper bag into strips. Billy tosses the iPad onto the sofa next to the bagged gifts and Christine *gah*s aloud.

"So where's Hai," her son says as he stacks the fallen gifts back on the sofa.

"You check under the beds?" Christine crawls to the fire, ribbons of paper bag in her fists, and bunches them up in the spaces beneath the wood logs, hoping the fake log can spread to them.

The door opens, and Billy looks outside with his back to the room. The Duraflame sucks the fire back into it. Where the bits of paper bag have started to burn, the edges turn from orange to black to smoke. "No, no," she says, waving, "it's not a cat door, you can't leave that open."

"You did," Billy snaps. "You stood here watching me like some zombie. Sure she didn't get past your legs?"

Derek's foot slips. His features go wide, eyebrow arching so high that the scar reaches out to hook you and pull you with—

"Uh-huh, just like that," Billy says. She squints a question mark at him, and he bugs his eyes, lets his jaw droop, and grunts. "You stood there, and you let the cat out when I got the firewood," he says. "And Dad's boots."

Clear as a bell she can picture Haiku shooting out around her as she chewed her lip and thought about her son getting taller and taller. But that doesn't mean it happened.

She pulls the trigger over and over before the lighter ignites, and she holds it to the longest strip of brown paper bag. "Just shut it, okay?" she says, and he slams it. "It's freezing out there. If Hai went out, she'll be meowing at a window any minute."

She sets the lighter behind her hip, and watches flame spread from one piece of paper to the next, start to lick up the side of the Duraflame again. It burns right next to one of the wood logs leaning on the fake one without catching. In Christine's mind's eye the pine trees glow brilliant green outside, and the oaks as well. The strips of paper curl up bright and orange, then uncurl back onto the ashy concrete. The flame from the strips turns into one flame, and licks at the rough-cut edge of a log. Jagged little splinters burn, and the fire spreads.

"Your mom's not totally useless, kiddo," she says.

"Gone…"

She whips around, not for a second thinking the voice is her son's.

Who's not even there. The fire crackles soft as wind. She calls his name, pops her head around the partition to make sure he isn't in the kitchen, then shoots down the hall to his tiny bedroom, hers. She runs back into his, checks the closet, which he'd barely even fit in—even if somehow the mood had hit him to play hide-and-seek.

"Three of us, and the trees…" the voice says.

And they're both gone, Billy and—

"Goddamn cat!" she barks, and runs for the front door.

Though she's less worried about her cat or her son than that the voice is back.

At least the snow has stopped, for now. A powdery shell covers the windshield and roof of the car. Christine yells her son's name over and over, stops in the middle of the winding little road that connects the cabins, and hugs herself against the dark cold that takes her breath away. She hunches, trying to jam her chin into the collar of her sweater, when she hears his voice. Her son's voice. For sure.

She can't make out the words, not so much because of distance, but because he's crying.

Christine runs around the back of the cabin to find Billy knocked to his bare knees in the snow. She throws herself at him, covers his back while she tugs at his shoulders to pull him up.

"What did you see?" she shrieks. An old toilet sits under a window of the house, the lids missing from both the bowl and the tank. Black leaves poke out, but the side of the house has mostly blocked the falling snow. At the edge of the trees a fat stump sits, much thicker than any of the trees around it, a short branch growing from the top. Nothing moves.

And her son sobs, "Haiku…"

He lets Christine pull him up, and she sees it. At Billy's knees. A pale gray knot stomped into the snow.

Nothing moves.

"What the fuck," he says, and she stops the urge to shush him. Christine wonders what could have taken all Haiku's teeth, but it's not the mouth she sees—it's an eye socket, one chartreuse eye missing. Ribs poke out like snapped white fingers, and the cat's ginger fur appears red, even in the moonlight, red. A short spool of intestine reaches across the snow. Christine chases away the thought that there should be more.

Billy says something about her leg, "Her *leg*," he says, a tremor in his voice. And the cat's leg pokes up, the paw bent in a wave, the only leg Christine can see at first. Two more are sunk into the snow. But Billy means the other hind leg, gone, the hip splintered so it's hard to even tell from the broken ribs that point up at Christine.

She closes her eyes, searches the trees again. Now she shushes her son, listening, for the voice, for the careful movements of the figure at the roadside last night.

The tree stump at the edge of the clearing, it isn't rooted to the ground. Someone put it there. The little branch twisting out of the top of the stump, the handle of a hatchet.

A hatchet didn't do this.

"We need to go inside," she whispers. When Billy shakes his head and blubbers, she says it again. Armentia warned of moose. And she'd brought up Stephen King's coke-addled trainwreck about an enormous rabid junkyard dog. A way-too-stupid idea finds purchase in Christine's brain and she's not strong enough to pull Billy to his feet but he doesn't resist and she leads him around the front of the cabin.

*No pets.*

So the bitch in the houndstooth pullover put a curse on them because she'd found out they'd brought a pet? Because their reservation was under Deerrek Sinclaire, not Missus?

"Deer-rek was your husband."

Christine shoves her son in the door, slams it against the voice, and hopes the voice stays out in the snow with the cat.

The cat bowl clatters into the sink. Kibble races around the drain like roaches.

Her messenger bag lies open, flat like an old encyclopedia on the kitchen table. Christine pulls books from two different pockets, squares the corners into a stack, and slips the middle-sized paperback out. The cover curls from years of love. She presses a palm over it, takes a long breath.

Without a word Billy had disappeared to his room. She pictures him under the covers, no plan to come out to say goodnight. Plinking away on his phone despite the wonders of nature all around. But the joke's on him—no Wi-Fi, except there *is* Wi-Fi.

*Minecraft* works offline.

The paperback cover shows an area chart in shades of orange and blue, jagged mountains under a white sky. The main text for her favorite analytics class, Christine still counts on *Datagraph* whenever starting a new project. The client, a Jersey investment group full of dudes just a few years younger than her, are the types that will respond to a lot of graphs.

The argument about what to do with the cat finally ended in a compromise. A draw, one might say. Billy had run inside and come back out with the buffalo blenkty, thrown it over the cat, and laid a couple sticks and a rock on top of it. All the funeral poor Hai would have for the night. Let the permanent record show that Christine Sinclaire's best moment of parenting came in convincing her son William that he could not dig a hole in mountain rock in freezing solstice temperatures.

A moose would not have partially eaten Haiku, though.

Pages flip past her thumb as she shakes her head. The book falls open to a spread near the back. Ants crawl across the States. A towering battalion of orange and gray patriots line up off the coast, brandishing pitchforks, wrenches, and shovels to take on the bugs. *Starship Troopers* meets *Aliens* meets *Land of the Giants*. Everybody knows insects love water, so the biggest knots of them cluster near the bottom of California, Texas, the Northeast. The chart tells the story of manual-labor occupations across the country, the black dots showing geographic distribution and the two-legged icons representing different jobs.

Billy could have interrupted a bobcat, and not noticed the miserable predator scamper off. In fact, he would've been calling Haiku's name, giving the thing plenty of notice. And thank god, too—no one needs to sneak up on a cougar in the middle of a meal. If it comes back out here behind the house, all that wool cover will do is keep the cannibalistic little shit warm while it feasts on a member of the family.

A black and white checkerboard marks Haiku's temporary grave. Only their footprints disturb the ground around it, coming and going in a messy path. Christine sucks in cold air, goes to pull her scarf tighter, but it's gone.

She hops backward at the sound of rustling, almost tripping through the snow—her eyes shoot to the toilet planter, her only question if the bobcat will shoot out of the tank or out of the bowl.

The sound comes from overhead, though, the leafless branches scratching at each other, giant, tuneless legs of cicadas.

Besides the sound overhead, just the wind. Nothing moves.

She should have grabbed gloves, how could she not think to grab gloves? The wool rectangle holds its shape—there must have been enough moisture in it to freeze solid. It makes no sense, a wool blanket, but it's like flipping over a sheet of plywood left in the yard all winter, to find snakes writhing underneath.

Christine only finds a mutilated cat.

She kneels in the snow. She doesn't say a prayer, but hopes that Hai, if looking down from above, will believe that she prays. The branches hardly make a sound as they scratch at each other.

The snow and the fur slice at Christine's fingers as she digs in under the side of the cat. She wedges her fingertips under the spine, still intact, to avoid the torn-apart belly. She tries to cup the cat, remembers cupping her as a kitten not that long ago. But the form doesn't bend into her hands. Not like Derek wrapped around the railing over the cellar stairs, fluid as any clock Salvador Dalí ever painted, a wax voodoo doll left on a radiator. Haiku is stiff as plywood, no less stiff than the sheet of wool. Blame it on freezing or on rigor mortis, none of the cat's three legs bend when they come loose from the icy grass, purple and blue under the solstice moon.

Christine carries the body at arm's length until she has to hold it against her hip to open the front door, her fingers red and throbbing. Then again when she pulls open the freezer door.

That goddamn glacial ice box.

So much ice.

It cakes all sides of the freezer. It had slipped Christine's mind. Ice pushes in from every direction, toward a crystalline space in the center barely big enough to shove Haiku's head inside of, much less her whole rigid body. At the grocery store Christine had made a quick pass of the pathetic frozen aisle, just grabbing the pizza she would heat up as soon as she got back to Cabin Eight. But she hadn't gotten any other frozen foods, because of the situation with the freezer.

So what did she think she was gonna do with the catsicle?

Haiku's three legs press up straight against Christine's ribcage. She's holding her feline family member the way she might hold a purse, or a football.

*Just the three of us and the trees.*

With both hands she gently sets Haiku on the Formica counter, but the cat still clatters like a dish dropped in a steel sink. She rests a hand on the poor creature, recalls stroking that ginger fur, a thousand times, going back years, just hours ago in the Toyota. It's not revulsion that jerks her hand away. The last thing she needs is her own body heat thawing the cat any faster.

She had pressed the palm of her hand on the back of the dull kitchen knife and rocked it back and forth to cut through the pizza. Bits of red and brown mar the knife's edge, and she doesn't rinse it before going to work on the ice floe in the compartment over the fridge.

The edge of the knife scrapes away the crystal center with ease, widening the central cavity. Having hit more solid ice, and with the blue dust piled up, Christine searches the cupboards for a bowl, finds a large plastic one, perfect for popcorn, and hugs it against her breasts under the open freezer door as she scrapes ice dust out into it. Some gets on her sweater, some on the floor, but she catches enough. She grinds the edge of the knife against the remaining ice, but it does nothing. She has to chip at it.

First with the edge, then the tip of the knife, she cuts at the ice with precise swipes and pokes, and the work goes a bit faster. To fit the cat, it's not like she'll have to stab all the way into the corners. The space she'll open can be more like an oval, an egg, a womb, rather than cleaning out every bit of ice from the entire cubic space. In gangster movies when they dig holes for their victims, you see two men leaning on shovels over a perfect sharp-edged hole clearly dug with a backhoe.

Even if she does clear every bit of ice, Haiku's long torso, those stiff legs—the cat won't fit as is. Christine stabs harder into the ice, imagining the blade severing her kitty's tail. Could she cut through the knees, or could she get away with removing the paws? Haiku's missing leg starts to look like a silver lining. For the three remaining limbs, it would probably work better to snap them, and fold them in against her torso, rather than cutting.

The tip of the blade skids across the ice.

If she cuts the cat up, she could use Tupperware, which would be better for the freezer. Especially if the ice pushes back in once Haiku's in there. She imagines having to do all this over again, hacking the cat free from freezer ice a few days from now, a gory capper to history's saddest Christmas.

Derek's foot slips—Christine reaches, everything she has, their fingers almost touch but the world explodes white. A blizzard shrieks, sucks the air from their lungs, seals their eyes closed, a fire extinguisher shooting ice instead of foam. The whole world disappears in a white moment.

Of course, the voice. Back.

Why does it call her "Mom?"

Watermarks stain a wall without windows or doors. A group of light bulbs stick out of the wall and Christine looks away from the two that shine. A third flickers and goes black.

And the knife sticks out of the side of her neck. She's glad she can't see that, would not look even if she could turn her head. Somewhere an angry snake hisses without pause.

Billy's voice, "Mom!" comes from behind the wall.

The shadows in the corners make better sense once she figures out the wall is not a wall, but the kitchen ceiling. One lit bulb in the fixture and three dead ones. The freezer door slowly swings shut, and the snake gets quiet, but doesn't stop.

She lies on her back. On the cold linoleum. Frost paints the top of the refrigerator door above her feet. She reaches for her neck, afraid that when she touches the blade it will hurt worse—but she finds only shivering skin, no cut. The sharp pain has to do with having fallen. The skin is so icy, though, she can't be sure she's alive. Because a fall can kill you.

Billy's face flickers between angry and worried as he leans in over her. The mustache makes the scowl more severe. The pale mist of his breath vanishes as soon as Christine sees it. She rubs at the kink in her neck. When her son looks up and away from her, anger takes over that face.

When did her baby become a man?

She pulls herself up to sit, and her own breath appears, but doesn't fade so fast. Beside her, a splash of water spreads out from an upside-down bowl. The knife sticks out from under the counter by Billy's feet, and her fingers tickle her neck.

Sounds follow the mist from Billy's mouth, but something stopped working that would let Christine put his words together. His mustache has faded to a hint of down. A long pink drip falls from the chrome edge of the counter, and Billy's arms jerk at his side as though someone has a hold of them, and she struggles to get up.

It may be that she can't process his words, if those even are words.

Blood pools around the cat on the green countertop—the dead don't bleed, so the cat must have been stunned, preserved in the ice. Christine climbs to her feet, yelps at Billy not to touch her, and she means Haiku, even though he'd made no move to do that.

He faces his mother, but she can't take her eyes off the cat. No blood flows from that mangled abdomen, those partially eaten organs. She is dead, for sure. The blood that had frozen into her fur has melted as the cat thawed.

Her son's eyes shift from anger to hatred with such subtlety, but still enough to let Christine look away.

In the fireplace, a few black chunks poke out of a cold blenkty of ash. Nothing burns.

# 5

Either in the room, or nearby, something rustles. The wind blows through hanging drapes, or a figure crawls out from beneath a sheet.

The thin mattress pinches under Christine as she sits up in bed and rubs her neck. She reaches out from under the cozy warmth and feels around the other side of the bed, Derek's side, for the cat. She listens for the noise that woke her but hears only faint bird calls.

Just the wind. Pale morning light filters in through the cracks in the blinds to illuminate the room just enough for her to make out the little four-paned window, the lamp on the nightstand, the simple dresser. Her suitcase sits undisturbed on the floor at the foot of the bed and the bedroom door hangs closed, the shadows lurking in the corners shallow enough to see through.

*Just the wind.*

71

Her eyelids droop, until another rustle snaps them wide. Not the wind.

She searches the shadowy corners of the bedroom for Haiku. The sun has barely risen. Sometimes the cat can sit so still, watching but not watching, that she blends right into the furniture.

Christine pulls the patchwork quilt up to her chin, swallows her heart back down when the noise stops. Her feet search around for the warm lump of ginger fur on top, the spot where Haiku always lies.

"Hai?" she calls. "Here kitty, kitty."

The sheets go cold on top of Christine and the chill turns her lungs into fists. She can't feel the weight of the patchwork blenkty against her numb toes. All sound leaves the room now except for the blood trying to press its way through her veins.

If she just hadn't dwelt on the cat, had not been so determined to find Haiku, maybe she could've gone the whole morning. A little bit longer, at least, before she had to recall her son carrying the body out to the backyard, and everything that followed.

Through the thin wall her son croaks out a call. "Mom," he says as though he can barely breathe.

She shoots to her feet, and her bedroom door bounces off the wall she hits it so hard, flinging his open with a bit more care.

The four-pane window in this room faces east, and

the light comes through the shade stronger. His phone is on the mattress next to him, and Billy's face glows across the pillow. He's tucked a fist under his cheek, and she's surprised to see a wrist so thin, the mustache barely a shadow under his nose, and he breathes just fine.

"Where are we?" he asks her without opening his eyes.

Her fingertips shoot up to her mouth, to lips icy to the touch.

"Wuh-we…" she stammers. "We're at a cabin, Daddy rented it for—" and her son laughs.

Billy opens his eyes and he laughs and rolls onto his back, pulling the patchwork quilt up to his chin. "I mean what *town*. What's the name of it?" he asks. "New York State, right? Or Massachusetts?" He cranes his neck around to take in the space without sitting up. "I woke up and it didn't look like my room."

Christine catches her own breath. "It isn't." She sits on the edge of the twin bed.

Her son laughs and yawns, throws his forearm across his face. "You know there's Wi-Fi?" he says. The word comes out garbled over the yawn, but of course he'd poke around until he found it. She hadn't come up with anything to tell him, and now her thoughts race away from her.

Billy says, "But it takes a password."

Birds call and answer in the distance. He reaches for her hand on her knee. With his eyes closed, he's not a boy

73

of fifteen, but twelve, now, maybe ten. He wiggles toward the wall to make room. She scoots against the headboard, covering his phone, and he uses her thigh as a pillow. He tugs the patchwork quilt under his chin. He doesn't ask why she's so stiff, and soon his breathing gets so soft and easy she knows he's asleep.

When he'd taken the cat off the counter, he'd said he thought dead things got stiff. With her brain spinning so fast, Christine hadn't known what he meant, said she left Haiku on the counter too long and *she defrosted*, because she couldn't think of the word *thaw*. But Billy had been thinking of rigor mortis.

Now that brow, those eyes, show no troubles or cares at all. Christine shrugs off the urge to start the day so she can soak up a little of her son's ease and contentment by osmosis.

The light through the window gets stronger before he rolls over, and she goes to make coffee. She distracts herself with a cold Pop-Tart, but after a minute of the kettle brewing she tries to pour, turning the pot upside down just to get half a cup.

In the fireplace, a few black chunks of wood stick out of the cool gray ash.

Christine changes back into yesterday's jeans and bundles all the way up, down jacket and gloves, grabs the car keys from the table by the sofa—she can't find the scarf—and crunches out into the snow. A tiny brown bird swoops out of a pine tree across the road, and others answer when it calls. The snow has piled up overnight, and what's slid off the roof has built up around the cabin. She doesn't even open the door of the Toyota. Snow has blown around the tires enough that she won't get any traction, won't be able to drive without digging it out. The way her eyes frost up, Christine can't imagine anything will melt anytime soon.

It's a short walk to the firewood stall, but she couldn't carry more than a few logs back. "Sounds like a job for two," she says, and wanders the other way down the twisting winter wonderland boulevard, under branches thick with white, wondering how many more structures there are past their Cabin Eight. Armentia had said the deluxe cabin, the fancy suite, was close to the office, so the road would have to loop around. Christine has cleared a couple bends in the road before she remembers the second key, on the flimsy plastic fob Armentia handed her. She should have grabbed that, but if she finds the other cabin, she can just look.

The road bends again, and someone stands in the road, reaching up to a pine bough that hangs low. She recognizes the slow, careful movement of the figure near the firewood stall last night. Christine sees him just as she hits the curve. His black eyes roll heavenward above great jutting cheekbones, so before he can notice her she scoots to the side and presses up against a fat, bare trunk. With her cheek so close, frost radiates off the bark.

She slinks around the other side of the tree. The wind moans like monks, and snow muffles any noise her feet make in the detritus of leaves, twigs, and branches on the forest floor. She creeps past one trunk at a time for a better view.

The figure eases its bulk around for a better angle on the fresh pine needles above. One moment the torso looks enormous, but then the bones seem to poke out. Last night Christine had seen it knock snow off overhead branches. A creature that appeared impossibly tall now spreads out to fill the width of the road as well. The canopy filters the daylight to a frozen morning gray, but it's enough for her to see the thing nod its head to clear snow from its antlers. The head nods side to side, the thick neck slowly bends one way then the other. Seen straight on, in the moonlight, she'd thought it human, tall and thin. From the side, it's even bigger. More dignified than she could see in the dark. She only notices the bird perched on its hip when it twitters away.

She'd never thought of an animal as majestic until this moment. She could run under the belly of the beast and barely need to duck—though one kick from those tree-trunk legs and she'd snap in—

She'd look like the cat they found out back last night.

Fat lips pick needles, slow but precise. You could teach a moose to type with those things. She pictures the jaw opening last night and presses her lips to the icy bark to muffle a gasp.

This thing ate her cat.

Her eyes frost over with tears, tear the skin from her face. Christine pulls her hands away from the trunk before they freeze there.

If Billy, if her sweet son, wakes up, he'll come looking for her.

*Just the three of us and the trees.*

The moose chews icy twigs with a soft crackle, lowers its head, stretching the branch down until it snaps.

Derek's foot slips. His features go wide, the hook-shaped scar soars over his eye, a black hole in his—

Branches slice into Christine's face as she crashes between the trees. She doesn't look for the road, only aims to put the thing directly behind her as far and fast as she can. Her ankle twists, but she stays up and pounds forward. A bend in the road works to her favor and she stomps the gas, sprinting through powder without looking back, her ankle screaming though she won't let it slow her down.

Her lungs hammer away. She times her footfalls with belly-deep gasps for breath. The air can't come fast enough, but the way it freezes at the bottom of her chest, that might be what stops her.

She slams into the trunk of the Toyota, and her elbows hold her up. The road behind her is clear, just her footprints coming and going. She tries for slow, deep breaths, but when she can't control it, she embraces the panic. She presses frozen cheeks against the snow and the smooth trunk beneath, the snow delicious in her mouth.

The moose *ate* the cat. She spits the ice on the trunk and gets to her feet, ankle on fire, arms still resting on the car.

The moose ate the cat, but at least a man did not eat her cat. If Haiku died under the hooves of a wild animal, it's tragic, it is in fact Christine's fault for letting her slip through the door—but it's also natural. She doesn't know why that is better, but she decides to believe it.

All she needs to do is treat the animal with respect. The word *regal* pops into her brain. You treat it with the respect it deserves, and keep your distance. Billy may not see it that way, since, let's face it, he loves the cat more than she ever did.

*Just the three of us and the trees.*

No amount of scraping helps clear the side mirror of the Toyota, and breathing on it makes it worse. She tries to see her reflection but decides she has to go in, no matter how red her eyes might be.

At least the figure didn't talk to her this time.

With her boots off, the other gear laid across the sofa, Christine limps back to find the sheets tossed around the foot of Billy's bed. She raps on the bathroom door, bends her knee to keep her bad ankle from touching the ground. Sometimes he won't answer right away, but he never ignores the second knock.

She pushes the door open to make sure he's not there. The chill starts to leave her skin as she stands in the middle of the den. The white dusting of snow doesn't fade from her jacket, her footprints hold their white shapes. It can't be very warm in here. She shuffles into her room to change her socks, moving slow as a moose around the bad ankle. Back at the sofa she pulls the rest of her gear back on. One by one, her hands, her feet, her throat begin to freeze again even before she heads outside.

She'd decided not to tell her son about the moose, and now he might be out here alone with it. The question forms in her brain, the sort of question that winds up in a meme.

She plants her butt against the driver's door and digs her phone from her pocket, slips a glove off to reach back in. The hand comes out with the laminated password card she'd found on the kitchen counter. Next to the coffee pot. She shoves her wallet back down into her pocket and opens Settings on her phone. The wheel spins as Other Networks fill in one by one by one. For sure Armentia couldn't just use cabin numbers. Christine matches a random string of letters and numbers to the one on the white business card, taps it, and thumbs in the password. Wind rustles overhead, and she stares down the road until her eyeballs freeze over. The network's moved up to the top of the screen, and she opens her browser and taps the bottom bar to type with one frozen thumb.

*do moose eat meat*

The phone suggests variants using *does*, *can*, and *will*, but she taps on hers.

A gray mass pulls her eye. Bigger than ever, the figure appears in the road. Christine jumps—the phone and card tumble to the snow. Her ankles cross mid-step, one of them screaming hot fire, and she crashes sideways. She twists to roll under the Toyota, but the snow blocks her.

Billy steps around the fender of the car, an armload of firewood piled up to his chin. Christine grabs her phone, comes up with a handful of snow. She shoves it all into the belly pocket of her down jacket. The hand comes out and shakes the ice off bright red fingers.

Some other hand seems to reach into her mind to yank her scrambled thoughts into one clear idea: Your son looks concerned instead of disgusted.

"I'm okay," she says, "I'm okay." Billy crouches beside her and sets down the logs, as she pushes herself to kneel, then stand, again with the help of her faithful steed and its strong trunk. "Phew," she laughs, "you got me!"

"I didn't mean—!" he stutters.

"No, no," she says. She hunches against the car as if to catch her breath. She crouches in the middle of the world's messiest snow angel. "I know, honey, it's just..." The password card has disappeared. "It's funny."

He sets a hand on the stack of wood. "I saw a hatchet last night, uh, around back," he says. "If I cut these down into smaller pieces it'll be easier to start a fire." He moves his hand over hers on the side of the car, rises to his feet, and gently tugs for her to follow. His legs show red rather than pink through the torn jeans.

"Good thinking, honey." She can't bring herself to say, *You remind me of your dad.* She scans for the password card again, but follows his black boots through the snow around the side of Cabin Eight.

Derek's foot slips…

*Deerrek was my husband.*

"Those fit okay?" Her voice cracks like a sitcom teenager. Teenage boy. When you follow someone, especially through the snow, it's only natural to watch their footsteps. She stretches out her stiff fingers. She dropped her glove, the one she'd pulled off to go through her pockets, and forgot to look for it when she couldn't find the card.

He tells her that the boots don't fit but he doesn't mind. She asks if he saw her scarf at the log rack when he—

Derek's foot slips on ice-slick asphalt shingles—the bottom of one boot flies up, obscuring his features as they go wide, one eyebrow arching up over the toe of the boot. An almost comical expression, the whites of his eyes blind her when they reappear under the foot.

Christine lunges for her husband's hand—her icy red fingers almost touch his, almost touch the green line that coils from his hand—but she gets nothing but air. The scar over his eye slams down as he winces, face scrunching—

*Snap.*

Christine stands alone in the woods, in the snow.

*Snap.*

Missing one glove. Alone in the woods next to a tiny house—the rented cabin, the place that Derek rented. Her arms tremble, not from the cold. Her legs too. Footsteps in front of her go around the corner to where they found—

Billy stands over a fat stump at the edge of the trees. He stands a smaller piece of wood on top. A hatchet hangs from his other hand.

She takes a long slow breath and says, "Thank you for doing this, thinking of it." He swings the hatchet. *Snap.* She jumps in place. The throbbing in her limbs reaches her brain. The head of the little axe digs into the top of the log but doesn't split it. She makes fists, tight as she can, to get the blood moving, to warm her frostbitten hand.

He raises the hatchet again, and it brings the log up with it. Billy's brow is knit, like whenever his dad would focus on a physical job.

"I was gonna drive down there," she says, "to the firewood stall." She hugs herself and flexes her thighs. "But you didn't see my scarf?"

"Nope." Quiet, focused, he swings with both hands, as though banging a nail with that hammerhead of a log.

The hatchet snaps through it. The kinder expression she'd noticed after she'd fallen beside the car: either it's gone or she'd imagined it.

He tosses the pieces onto the gray and white buffalo blenkty beside him, sending up a little cloud of fine white dust. The pieces clatter against three skinny pieces of another log he's already split, then he grabs another thick chunk from the small pile behind him.

"I was going to drive," she says, "but there's no getting out of that snow out front."

Billy sets the log across the stump, doesn't stand it upright. His face darkens. Her arms fill with fire and her pulse hammers behind her eyes.

"We didn't bring chains." He doesn't turn to her when he says it, not at first. "Did you forget chains?" Now he looks at her. Not out of the corner of his eye. Head on. Her arms and legs twitch. She tries to remember how much coffee she's had.

"Stop it!" she shouts, pounding her fists at her side. "I'm trying, Billy!" Does his grip choke up on the hatchet? She steps back toward the corner of the cabin. Her legs wobble and her foot, it slips in the snow, but she doesn't go down. The blood flows again but brings little relief. "You think this isn't hard for me?" she shrieks.

He thwacks the hatchet into the top of the trunk.

"I know you wish it had been me," she says, "I know you wish I'd died instead of your dad." Derek never would've

forgot chains. "But I don't deserve this. It's not my fault—
and it's not fucking fair for you to hate me!"

He lunges at her. She's glad he put the hatchet down.
The blanket, the blenkty, it snaps underfoot.

"I don't hate you!" His face twists, mouth a black hole.
"I hate *him*!"

Her arms fly out, she does not know what she means
to do, to hug him or to push him away, but icy fingers
swipe across Billy's face and his head snaps backward.

She only catches his eyes for an instant, but he's Medusa
and she freezes in place, her claw suspended in the air
between them. His face glistens in the dim morning light,
cheeks the color of ice above a shiny crimson chin. He
reaches for the hatchet, and Christine doesn't want to run.

It should have been her, not Derek, it should have been
her instead, now together, a family, they can make that
right, half-right.

No force on earth, not even revenge, not matricide, will
make her son—her sobbing, bloody son—face her. He
shows her his back, he raises the hatchet overhead, brings
it down on the log laid crosswise over the trunk—

*Snap!*

"I'm sorry," Christine says, "Oh my god, Billy," she says,
"I didn't mean to—"

*Snap!*

He grabs the twisted log and tries to stand it upright,
but the gashes he just put in it make it impossible. He

spins and throws it—she gets a flash of his twisted face but her body clenches like a fist. She ducks. The chunk of wood smashes against the backside of the cabin nowhere near her, leaves a crack in the siding.

Billy stands another log on the trunk, strikes a superhero pose, hatchet above his head, those black wet-weather boots better than shoulder-length apart.

Derek's foot slips. The hook-shaped scar over his eyebrow arches. His features go wide. Eyes flash white, and Christine lunges—his hand still grips a line of Christmas lights. The green wire curlicues through the air as he swings for purchase, tiny dark bulbs clicking against each other.

She stretches her fingers, extends her arm, but she can't reach him, or the line of Christmas lights, cannot reach the hand. Grips. Nothing but air.

The sole of one boot flies up. White mountain pines arch over their cabin. He looks at her from under that black boot as he leaves the roof, head and shoulders first.

Toward their son. Billy stands in the tiny yard behind the house, behind Cabin Eight, a hatchet in one hand, dead cat clutched in the other. Blood and tears stream from Billy's face, his parka glistens bright blue streaked with purple, the gray blenkty draped over his shoulders.

A tall figure steps out of the woods behind him, giant knees creaking as it comes. The twisted bones that ring the figure's head knock snow from the branches, dusting the

LINDY RYAN

shoulders, the long, thick back—a torso so massive it would crush her son if it passed too close, snap every bone.

Christine, she races across the rooftop to the spot where Derek slipped, she freezes in place, hand suspended in the air before her. A green bullwhip loops through the air over Derek as he falls headfirst. His shadow turns the iron rail black, over the stairs to Cabin Eight's basement. Christine and Billy watch, frozen in place. Billy didn't see this. Billy was not home.

Derek snaps the black iron rail, his neck snaps it. The weight of all of him. His neck snaps it, then his shoulder snaps it, the thick iron folds under his weight coming straight down. He pulls the red iron bar, down into the sunken stairwell where he bunches up like a jacket thrown at the bottom of a cubby, and Christine's foot slips.

Frosted pines slash through the clouds. The white on a white sky goes quiet, until the faint music of birds returns.

Derek steps over to her, tall as a pine tree, hatchet in hand, neck twisted in a terrible question mark. Christine's head throbs. Derek's hangs from a thread, bobbles at the end of a shredded tendon, and he says—

"Mom." He says, "I'm sorry, Mom." Billy asks, "Are you okay?"

He crouches, red knees poking out. One arm hugs his shins, hugs the tops of his boots. He sets the hatchet down. A little hatchet-shaped snow angel presses into the snow.

And another hand reaches into her brain to soothe the pulse that beats there. She comforts herself that the Medusa's face shows a bit more concern than hatred.

# 6

Billy yanks one off, the boot, his father's boot. A little flurry of snow dusts the floorboards in front of the sofa. He rubs his knees, leans back beside her and sighs at the rough rafters. Close, not because he wants to sit beside her, but because they never moved the Christmas presents off the couch.

Her son, just another man coming in after a morning's work gathering firewood. He takes a load off, feet sore, back perhaps stiff. He bends his leg and gets the other boot up on his knee, another little snowstorm. He works it off with both hands, drops it with the first one. His father's boots.

*Oh, no*, she says to the hostess in the houndstooth pullover. The scotty dogs across her chest tilt their heads in unison, cock a dozen little ears. *Oh, no, my husband isn't late*, she says, *he won't be joining us at all.*

Christine is not in the office, though, not talking to Armentia, but on the sofa with her son in the cabin that her husband rented for them.

*I'm sorry, I thought you said my late husband.*

The buffalo blanket is missing from the back of the sofa, and she hopes Armentia won't charge them for it. It's just outside, stiff as a board, same as their cat. A tiny system of lakes darken the floorboards around the black boots.

As Billy had helped her back inside, Christine gathered enough focus to search the spot where she must have dropped the little card with the Wi-Fi password. The fresh snow swirled across the ground in a white kaleidoscope that chewed the laminated card to sparkly plastic bits.

"I think I need a glass of water," she croaks.

Billy uncrosses his legs so hard the bottom of Christine's belly snaps like a whip into her throat. He could've cracked his stockinged heel the way it came down on the wood. The heel is the largest bone in the foot, she remembers, which just sounds like it's asking for it.

Outside, no bird sings. He must have left the cat somewhere? Back under the blenkty?

His foot, Derek's foot slips, his features slip, jaw unhinging like a python...

Billy holds out a glass of water. He stands in front of her in his socks. She can't tell anything from his face, no concern, but at least no hatred, maybe. That's fine, his wishes don't matter anymore, it's enough that she wants it now, that Christine wishes she had died instead of his father.

Around the boots there's no water, just a darker shade of floorboard. Billy holds the glass, a plate in his other hand. When he bends to set the glass on the bookshelf next to the sofa, she sees the plate. He takes his peanut butter on untoasted bread over to the dinette table and sits in the pale glow of single bulb.

Shadows knit splintery ceiling beams together, a tangle of black and brown and gray. She breathes deep, but it's not mountain air in here. In Cabin Eight the air is thick with mold. Water also darkens the floorboards around the pile of wood just inside the door. Her son will build a fire soon, she's sure, and it's bound to brighten the room a little bit.

The color's even seeped out of the wrapping paper. She touches one of the loose gifts on the pile beside her. Her son got her a book, she guesses. Her fingernail stabs under one corner of the auburn paper, and the little piece of tape there snaps, tears color off the paper to show white beneath. She peels a ribbon of the paper away. It's okay to use it if Billy needs help starting the fire, because they make gift wrap to recycle now. She hopes he didn't get her a copy of *Datagraph: The Story of Analytics in Pictures*. She grabs a handful of the paper, pulls it back to reveal shiny white cardboard beneath.

"Mom, what the hell?"

Billy leans over her and tears the last of the paper away from the white iPad Pro box. The paper falls to the wet spot on the floor, the words *From Mom and Dad* upside down in black Sharpie.

She tells him he's welcome, maybe out loud, though maybe not.

A less than superhuman effort gets her to her feet.

She tells him she's sorry. "Hey," Christine says. "We need to get something to eat." She takes a long, slow breath. "How long has it been?"

Billy drops the piece of bread on the pale blue plate. The way he wipes his hands sounds a little like applause.

Christine picks up the board and unwraps the pair of tea towels that cover it. Grooves swirl across the wood surface like the filigree in a decorative railing. She hadn't wrapped it to protect the board, but to protect everything packed around it in the trunk. Spikes thicker than soccer cleats stab up from the wood. Derek had brought the spiked cutting board to the marriage. It clatters from her hands onto the counter.

Billy looks over from the dinette table. He exhales as though he'd held the breath a long time, as though he's just avoided a crash. He averts his eyes, but just barely. Christine feels watched. Every move she makes, every noise, he jumps a little. She knows she rattled him, acting the way she did. Billy takes the corners of a small plastic package and pulls it apart, peels off slices of roast beef.

"See the grooves?" she asks. He looks over again. Christine traces a finger across the scarred wood surface of the cutting board, careful of the spikes. "They drain the juice from the meat to a single point at one end of the board. I try to pop that end over the sink, but the way they made this counter…"

Every new place they moved into, Derek would find a place for the cutting board in some high cupboard, some out-of-the-way kitchen cabinet, so when she needed it she'd ask him to climb up, though he wasn't much taller than her. And he'd pull it down, do his best Marlon Brando, *Look how they massacred my board*. The board had entered the marriage with few scars. Now fine brown lines crisscross the surface, more than a spiderweb, more than cracked glass, more like an entire nervous system pulsing under the clear plastic skin of an invisible man model.

She says, "It's the only piece of kitchen gear we kept from your dad's bachelor days."

"What did you do with the rest?" Billy lays slices of roast beef flat on the bread where he's already spread mayo. A glop of white pins the butter knife to the tabletop between the plates.

"Back to Goodwill," she says. "Mismatched silverware, cups, and dishes." She pulls the pork shoulder, wrapped in plastic, across the counter. With the eight-inch Wüsthof blade from home, she slices the little square of tape she'd used to fold the jumbo Ziploc bag around the meat. The tip nicks the bag. Not like she planned to reuse it, except maybe for the bone—the thought of leaving that out for the moose sends a shiver through her, head to toe.

"Your dad had this one frying pan." She hopes Billy didn't notice the twitch. "He lost the screw that held the handle. So he'd wound a piece of wire, like, in and around and around. If the frying pan had anything in it you couldn't pick it up, he'd just slide it off the burner."

She unseals the Ziploc, shimmies it down over the slab of pork the way you strip off a pair of tights, and slices through the plastic wrap the meat came in. She peels that away and inhales, surprised that she smells more mayo than ham.

Billy stands beside her in his socks. He holds out a plate with a sandwich on it. She set him to work on the dinette table after she covered the counter with holiday feast prep.

"Oh, thank you, honey," she says, but waves her hands, already damp. "Leave it on the table? Go ahead and eat. But watch, okay?" She bunches up the plastic and throws it in the sink, then scoops up the shoulder in both hands and drops it on the cutting board, wobbling it to set it on the spikes. "We'll prep it today, then eat Christmas Eve."

Billy talks around a mouthful of bread, mayo, ham. "What 'bout Christmas Day?"

"This here is eight pounds of fine pork shoulder, my man, so it could feed maybe ten people. I thought we'd eat it Christmas Eve and Christmas Day." She cranes her head around, searching the counter, kind of overdoing it. "Where is it," she says, "where is it...?" Billy just looks irritated, doesn't ask. But he watches her do her bit as he chews. The mayo paints it all white in there.

She reaches behind the big roasting pan on the counter and pulls out a small unlabeled deli container.

"Aye, there's the rub," she says.

She peels back the lid and tells him, "I roasted this at home." The brown powder sparkles as she pours it into the little white bowl. "Salt, brown sugar, garlic powder, citrus zest," she says. "Coriander seeds, fennel."

"Garlic?" he sneers.

"That's all you heard. Great." She finds the pestle and grinds the powder into a finer powder. Her ankle throbs. "I roasted it at home, but have to make sure it hasn't clumped together."

She leans over to rinse her hands, just cold water. "I think between the ride and being in this cabin, the rub has chilled enough." She searches the counter and takes one of the tea towels to dry her hands. "This next part is kind of gross," she says, "but kind of great." She pours a handful of the rub into one palm.

Christine grinds the handful of spices into the slab of pork, cups the other hand beneath to catch anything that falls, then rubs both hands across either side of the shoulder. "You have to make sure to get it all over. Thick!" The cutting board shifts a little on the counter, and she presses one hand on top of the meat while the other rubs, and then switches. "Leftovers on Christmas Day will save us—me—from cooking on the holiday itself. And don't worry. I got plenty of stuff to tide us over 'til then." She wrenches the pork off the spikes and flips it. "This'll cook all day tomorrow."

She presses it back down onto the board, then pours the rest of the mortar onto the clean side of the meat. Spices fill the punctures left by the spikes, and she moves her hands around until the wet surface feels dry from the grit. "All the time you put into prep, it just makes the meal more special. For the holiday. So it's worth it. And really, it's like an hour's worth of prep, and a whole lot of letting it sit." She yanks the pork off the spikes and turns it in her hands, then sets it back on the board, most appealing side face up. "The skin is already off, or I would have had to take it off. Only a real serious butcher would sell it with the skin on, and I got this at Market Basket, so, easy."

Billy walks over and sets his plate on top of the ball of plastic wrap in the sink, then stands beside her. She reaches under the hanging cabinets for the Saran Wrap, pulls off a long strip, and clears a spot next to the cutting board. "So now it'll go in the fridge overnight."

She lifts the meat off the board and sets it on the plastic. She washes her hands with dish soap this time. "You wash your hands a lot when handling raw pork, okay? Then tomorrow, seven hours in the oven." Christine looks at the old-school LED readout on the oven. "Jeez. What do you think?" Billy shrugs, having no opinion on out-of-date appliances—but he follows her every move, even as Christine dries her hands. "Well, ovens don't always go right at the temperature you set them at. The one in Columbus, I'd set it ten degrees low or else it'd burn everything." She wraps the plastic around the meat, smoothing it down with the same movements with which she'd rubbed in the spice. "So who knows with this, but that's the beauty of slow roasting." She opens the fridge and goes to hold the door with her hip, but her son steps around to get it. She smiles at him, grabs the wrapped meat, and places it on the shelf inside. "Err on the low temp side and check often."

She fishes out the roll of Reynolds Wrap from the counter, rips off two sheets, and lays them in the bottom of the roasting pan, thumbing them into the corners. "Then I'll just unwrap it, put some water down here, slap the meat on this thing, and cover it all with more foil." She drops the roasting rack on top of the tinfoil and pushes the rack and pan under the suspended cabinets. "Then we use the water from the pan to baste it as we go."

"Sounds good to me, Mom," her son, her Billy, he says.

Christine checks her hands. Clean and dry. She drums her fingers on the counter next to Billy. If she follows his eye line, she'd think he's admiring her work with the tinfoil, but she sees just enough of his pupil to know he's locked her in his peripheral.

The past few months, Derek has slipped into any silence that fell between them. Now her late husband is joined by his goddamn cat.

"Hey," she says, and touches his hand. "Remember why you used to call it a blenkty?"

"Mom, you should eat," Billy says.

She slaps her forehead, and laughs, sits at the table. She peels back a corner of the bread.

"What?" Billy asks.

She shakes her head, "Nothing," she says, "just checking how much mayo. You did it perfectly." She'd set out a package of sharp cheddar slices, but he didn't use them. Hidden someplace on the counter, probably.

"But blenkty," she says. "You don't remember?" She takes a bite and smiles at him as she chews. "You weren't even two. You'd spread a box of a thousand Crayolas around the living room."

"I don't think they come that big," he says, and she nods.

"Maybe the house near Seattle?" Christine says. "I asked you over and over to clean up, and finally I said, *William Thomas Sinclaire! Put every one of these away!* And you said, *Why you say me William—my name Billy!*" She covers her mouth. "You were so mad! When I stopped laughing, I put the crayons in the box, and explained that Billy is the affectionate version of William. That when I was little, they called me Chrissy."

"You mean diminutive," he says.

"Very good," Christine says around a mouthful. "But you were like eighteen months, what would you do with *diminutive*?

"I knew *affectionate*?" he says.

"Easier to explain." He laid the mayo on thick, and it brings out the salt of the roast beef. She swallows and tells him, "When you asked what they called your dad when he was little, you got so mad when I said there was no affectionate version of Derek." And it's like her husband is just in the other room, about to walk in any moment. "After that, you had to name any pet we got," she says. "Cookie, and Snowy, and a little brown mouse called Pepsi. Your dad made fun of you for naming the terrier Scotty even though it was a Boston." She chuckles. "That one was my fault."

"Oh my god!" he says, spitting into the sink, then spits again.

She asks what. He holds the empty deli container in his hand. Aye. "What did you do?" she asks.

He spits again, holds up a finger as if testing the air. "I just wanted to taste it. It's awful!" He sticks his tongue out and winces.

One clean swipe runs through the dust that clings inside the container. "It's not awful, you cook it into the meat," she tells him, as he makes more gagging sound. "It's not cookie dough."

He spits in the sink as she takes the last bite of her sandwich, wipes her hands together.

Billy says, "I had a blanket." Around the last mouthful she makes a face that asks *what*. "A blanket," he says again, "that I carried everywhere. Told people it was my imaginary friend."

"Even though it was right there." Christine reaches into her pocket, remembering a stick of gum. Maybe the taste will get him to stop spitting.

"We'd moved," he says, just like she would have said, "and I was mad that I had to leave my friends. I don't even remember their names." Neither does Christine. "But I knew I just imagined that Blenkty was a friend. Would that have been Washington?" She can't remember when she hurt her ankle either.

She says, "We left Washington for Alaska." Feeling around, she's careful not to pull the Wi-Fi password card out by mistake. She can't remember which pocket it's in, but the gum, she'd put that in the wallet.

He says, "Jeez. So I named the blanket." He spits in the sink again.

"Blenkty," Christine says. "You really need to keep doing that?" She pulls her wallet out and unfolds it, exhales when she doesn't see the Wi-Fi card inside. But where...?

"What happened with Haiku?" Billy asks, and the image of the shredded cat stabs at her. How could he forget that? He says, "Why didn't her name end with a Y?" Maybe he saw the look on her face.

"Your dad," she says. The silver wrapper on the stick of gum is faded, but pokes out from the middle of the wallet. "He gave you so much shit about all the cutesy names. You'd literally tried to name her Cutesy. When you said *Haiku*, I think you were just putting sounds together."

She pulls the silver stick of gum out, and a little square of paper falls. Too dark, too yellow to be the Wi-Fi password. The folded piece of paper lands between her son's feet on the linoleum floor.

"I didn't know a lot about Japanese poetry," Billy says. She holds the gum out to him, but he bends to pick up the paper. Better not be the password.

"Not yet," she says as he unfolds it. "So you made a sound that I turned into Haiku."

The expression leaves her son's face. And he doesn't look at her, and the stick of gum flashes as it falls to the floor. She knows it's not the Wi-Fi password, but the blurry, dimpled, tearstained obituary.

Billy wears that nothing expression, not quite slack, though soft. When he stopped ricocheting from rage to sorrow, when his face no longer stretched one direction

100

and then the other in the wake of his father's death, Billy's face fell into the not-quite-slack nothing that stares now at Derek's obituary. With the anger and the sobbing the boy had cried out for help, but when it passed his face said *leave me to this, don't come close.* And that distance opens up again as Christine feels the floor tilt under her feet and gravity suck her away from her son, and this time the room dissolves in black.

Again the first thing she hears is the sound of rustling.

The rock-hard mattress hurts every inch of her, cold through her clothes. She reaches around for the blenkty, even a sheet, and her fingertips skitter over the smooth surface under her. The floor. The birds make no noise. Just wind outside. Christine opens her eyes, but they're already open, still inside that black dissolve.

Something rustles, and she says her son's name, and he says, "Right here," and touches her leg. Her ankle throbs.

"Is this real?" she says, only as she notices a pale blue rectangle from the direction of his voice.

A shape eclipses the window, her son's head. "The power is out," he says. "What did you…" he starts to say, and trails off in a grumble.

"I didn't do anything," she says, and rolls on her side to sit. Touches one foot to the floor with care.

"Think," he says, "what did you *think*, but never mind."

She's surprised she can see him as he gets to his feet. One hand goes behind him and comes back fiddling with something, and his phone's light flashes across the living room. It fills out the edges of shapes, under-lights his face as he studies the room. He crosses, silent in his stockinged feet. She raises her own hands to check for all her fingers. Billy clicks the phone off and kneels in front of the fireplace.

"Billy, you were right, honey," she says to his back, his head dipped below his shoulders. "We shouldn't have come. I mean, *I* shouldn't have."

The fireplace makes sharp cracks like the snap of a whip. "I would've had a hard time getting here alone," he says, as he breaks skinny pieces of wood in his bare hands, maybe over a knee.

"You and your dad." She climbs up to all fours. "If it was me. If I fell off the roof," she says, "he would sure as hell have remembered chains." She crawls toward him. His elbows jerk at his sides. The hatchet lies next to him, but he doesn't use that. He snaps another piece of kindling. Christine's hands and knees move in sync, and she thinks of the treads of a tank.

She pops to her feet and lunges at her son, grabbing sticks from his hands.

He tries to grab them back. He says, "I'm gonna light—"

She blurts out, "Your dad!" and fights with him for them. "He did this one time!" She gets the kindling away from him and grabs more from the floor. Billy raises his hands in confusion. "Just like shitty little branches of pine," she says, waving sticks around. "From a pine tree. You lay them down," she says, jerking the armload of wood around. "Under the tires. Like railroad ties, or—" She struggles to her feet in the indoor twilight. "Or tank treads. Instead of slipping across the snow, the tires grab these, and you can drive. We'll go home!"

He looks like his dad, arguing, "What, lay down sticks all the way to New Jersey?"

Christine backs toward the door. "They plow up here," she says, "we just get to the road." She presses her body against the wall to keep the wood from falling as she fumbles with the doorknob.

She's wins him over when he grabs an armload of wood and he asks, "What if it's not plowed?"

She kicks his boots toward him. His father's boots. "I don't know," she says.

Billy lets go of the wood, kindling crashing across the floor, and drops to his butt, pulls the boots on. "If the hostess is there," he grunts, "she can give us the internet password and—"

"She already gave it to us." Christine blurts it out as she jerks the door open, a frigid blast of air rushing in. It's near broad daylight outside, but the trees block the cabin.

And her son stares at her. "What?" he says as he gets the second boot on and gathers the wood.

She says, "I mean of course she will." When he reaches for the hatchet by the fireplace, she adds, "Grab the keys."

Her son bares his teeth. "You said—"

"She already gave it to us!" she shouts and bangs the stack of wood against the door. "This little card, on the kitchen counter." She jerks her head toward the Toyota as she limps out onto the steps. "Get the keys, Billy. I didn't want you spending the whole time—"

"Jesus, Mom!" he shouts. He snatches the keys off the skinny table by the sofa, but just stares at her from the door.

"Billy, stop it," she says. "Just shut the—"

Christine's foot slips. The side of her explodes and the sky burns white. Not gray. Her features go wide, eyebrow arching, her feet, both feet, they fly out from under her. Wood tumbles through the air, bangs against the side of the house as her son turns upside down, features so wide, flits through her field of vision.

*Door*, she was going to tell him to shut the door.

His upside-down eyes swirl, round as suns. She can't hear whatever words Billy screams, but he sees it too, he sees this.

The antlers float over the thing's head as it rears up, tall as any pine tree. A neck thick as any oak. The hooves smash down on the hood of the Toyota, and a tire pops, spraying snow in Christine's face, and the smell of the creature stings her eyes, like a dog that's lived in a swamp its whole life. She's surprised how fast she gets to her feet with the pain stabbing up one leg. Billy hops from the stairs over the railing, the wobbly wood railing, which would just fall away harmlessly if you fell, say, twenty feet on it. He lands next to her in a superhero crouch, keys sticking out of the fist he raises at his side.

Christine's hands race around under her and come up with two lengths of firewood, long and thin as her forearm. She pitches them at the head of the thing—the first hits just under one black, rolling eye, and the other glances off an antler. It is what Derek would have done. If it was him here instead. If only it was him. The moose, the thing, it digs its fingers into the hood of the car and yanks it off like stripping a blanket off a bed.

# 7

She drags Billy by the hand as his scream reaches through the fog in her brain, her ankle screaming too. The moose, the thing, it crashes after them.

Billy pulls her toward the road and she jerks his hand, spins him sideways and he yelps.

"The trees," she yells, "between the trees."

She drags through spiny little branches that lash at her face, her eyes, her hair. She looks back, and her son's eyes are closed, and the thing charges at them, the thick legs bending differently now—is it even a moose at all? A cloud thick as smoke bursts from its snout.

They race into the trees, the three of them, hoofbeats like thunder.

She puts up a hand to part the branches that whip at her. She can't spare the breath to tell her son to do the same, hopes Billy can figure it out. In the freezing air their hands run slick with sweat, and she digs her fingernails into his palm so she won't lose him.

The snap of wood on wood rings overhead, and she glances back. The antlers, the creature's rack, cracks against the thicker branches up high. This slows it down. Perfect.

Her son squeezes her hand. Her shirt tugs, pulls off her shoulder, and Billy's grabbed her sleeve with the other hand. His steps are unsteady, wild. His dad's boots don't fit him.

"The thicker trees," Christine gasps, "it can't follow." Not as fast, anyway. It crashes through branches, raining pine needles around and behind it. On the road it would stomp them like some roadkill cat.

The trees get closer together, and that's how she loses his hand. Billy shrieks, "Mom!" and she tells him to run alongside her.

She forces herself to slow just enough that he's in the corner of her eye, and she yells, "Faster!" He pours it on, gets ahead. Somehow she manages a laugh. Derek's black boots fly across the snow and Billy's fists pump at his side as he runs. She limps after as fast as she can.

Christine stretches her fingers out to the side, toward him, extends her arm, but she can't reach her son. Like his father falling from the roof and dying instead of her.

But she can't go back, she can't trade places with Derek, no matter how much she wants it.

Her wrist slams into a thin trunk. It spins her around. The moose, the monster, the goddamn devil, it still races after her and her son, the three of them, in the trees.

She gets her feet straight under her again and sprints. Head down, she scans the corners of her vision, flails her hands out, grips nothing but air. The antlers crack through branches overhead, too close for her to stop and look around to catch sight of her son. Too loud to hear his footfalls.

The ground drops away. Her feet pedal through the air, and the pain in her ankle vanishes—but only for a second before she hits, and gravity takes her faster down the hill. She almost crashes into a trunk, and pivoting, she sees behind her—nothing coming. The crash of the antlers has stopped but she doesn't know when. The trees become further apart, and she lets one stop her.

The trunk knocks the wind out of her as green needles cover her. Christine digs her nails into the bark, harder than her son's hand, and lets the pine tree hold her up, balancing on one foot. Her lungs hammer away and she tries to slow it, but just wants as much of the cold air as she can get. She reaches overhead, grabs a branch, and uses it to turn herself around and settle her back against the trunk.

No birds sing, and nothing moves. The slope is still. She traces her own tracks—not footsteps, but a scattering of branches and snow—up to the crest, where she sees no farther.

She spins around, still leaning on the trunk, when a rustling comes from downhill. A bird, maybe an owl, flies out of a thicket of tall reeds and weaves between trees, then disappears. The ground sparkles between the reeds and brown grass. A voice whispers from below. As her own breathing slows, she can hear it better, but cannot make out any words. She steps away from the pine tree, toward the marsh, toward the voice. Without the thing chasing her, she steps with care. Twigs bend under her feet, beneath the snow. Light sparkles off the water. The lights had gone out in the cabin.

She hobbles down the hill, just her and the trees. She can't make out the words, but the voice welcomes her down.

Under her bad ankle, a branch snaps beneath the snow. It cracks like the antlers crashing, snapping, through trees.

She spins and shoots up the slope, and she screams her son's name at the top of her lungs.

An echo from the marsh behind her calls her name, that voice, "Christine..."

Trees fly past her, branches slice her face—she's sure she's closing on Cabin Eight when suddenly the trees around her vanish and her feet stomp through powdery snow on the flat open roadway.

Not the highway, but the road between the cabins and the office. She missed her cabin, but it can only be this way. Or that—

The road bends so Christine can only just make out the shape—the big rectangle of wood with the figure rearing up and down in front of it, its rack brushing the pine boughs overhead, hooves kicking up a cloud of snow like smoke. The forelegs stomp the ground in front of the plastic doghouse below the billboard, stomp the figure lying there, its arms and legs dancing. The light bulb above the firewood stall highlights the forelegs that punch her son into the snow, stomp on his chest, where she imagines his torso and head hide in the flying white. The light reflects off the Plexiglas that covers the flyers. Her son's legs kick out, almost comical in their dance. The bottom of one boot flies up, and Christine's features go wide, the whites of her eyes freezing blind.

If Derek's foot had not slipped, if she had died instead and he were here, he would run at the thing, body slam it across that doghouse and through the plywood backing, if he were here, if she had fallen instead.

*I'm sorry it was your dad that died, instead of me.*

She just leans into a trunk along the edge of the road. The birds are quiet. She extends one arm, stretches her fingers, but she can't reach her son, touches nothing but air. She would do anything to spare him, but she's too far, just as she was too far from Derek, almost the whole roof between them, the green line of Christmas lights spooling off his hand a million miles from her as he fell in the other direction.

The monster rests its feet on the red patch of snow and glares down the road at Christine, black mouth open in a silent scream. It drops its antlers and flares the whites of its eyes before breaking into a gallop, and Christine, she sprints, her ankle's killing her but she sprints back through the forest.

Dodging trees, she makes sure to run in a straight line, keeps the road behind her. Even with the antlers smashing through branches behind her, she won't panic. A wooden limb slashes right across her eye, and she tramples with the one eye closed without letting up. Her lungs throb hot and cold at the same time, her blood way up but the air freezing in her chest. She limps around one huge trunk, wider than her, and leans back against it. She'd lost the sound of the moose's rack as her own footfalls got louder. Now she can barely hear the antlers over her own breathing. The thing must be further away and, she thinks, moving more slowly too. She looks back the way she came, and makes a hard turn, ninety degrees, so now she creeps along, parallel to the road—assuming the road runs straight, but it curves away from her at the firewood stall. She can keep a straight line, not having to run. She leans into another trunk, letting her ankle float, throb, off the ground. The sounds of the forest swallow any noise the monster makes, branches just shifting around her in the wind. No birds sing.

With another turn, Christine heads to the road, and she sees the tall shape of the wood wall. She approaches from behind, so the wall blocks her view of the doghouse, and the bloody spot in the snow. Her feet get tangled in bramble hidden in the snow, and she pulls them free, breathing shallow little breaths so the loudest noise is the blood in her ears. She doesn't want to see that red snow on the other side of the wood structure, but she has to see it. Has to see the body.

She digs her fingernails into soft pine bark and listens. If the creature's rack bangs against branches, it's far away. With Billy dead, not ten feet from her now, and the thing not chasing her, it wouldn't be running at all. She searches the road beyond the firewood stall. Maybe when she hobbles out from behind the wood structure, she'll see the monster waiting for her.

Just as well. It should have been her instead. Instead of anyone.

The lightbulb glows. It was off when she came here the day before, but it's been fixed. It reflects off the Plexiglas, a splash of blood running up toward the bulb from the mess on the ground. The flyers are painted red.

The voice she hears now belongs to Derek. And she laughs, she can't help it.

His best Marlon Brando.

*Look how they massacred my board.*

The boots that stick out from the end of the bloody mess at her feet, the boots aren't Billy's. They aren't Derek's either. Broken legs twist this way and that up to the bottom of the red coat, soaked red with blood to obscure the cartoon terriers, the houndstooth pattern.

A jagged crack like a lightning bolt runs across a face with one gray eye. Blood pools in the other eye cavity, and what remains of the lipless mouth runs in a thin, diagonal line. Her torso, which Christine remembers as stout, lies flat as a frozen buffalo blenkty in the snow. The monster shredded the top of the houndstooth sweater, tore it away to show bits of bones like so many fingers floating in the red pool of her chest.

It found more of a meal in Armentia than in Haiku. Had she come to fix the billboard light? Had she dealt with the power outage in the cabins?

Rather than turning Christine's stomach, the ruined guts tell her one thing—it didn't get her son.

She kneels in the red snow beside the body and pulls open the pocket of the pullover, slides her fingers through the sticky gap to find a tube of ChapStick snapped in half. She reaches across, slips her hand into the other pocket, and pulls out a fat bunch of keys on a chain of rings. The smashed fob falls away when she touches the keys. One stands out from the rest, with a hard rubber Ford logo on the end of the key. She'll find Armentia's pickup if she gets back to the office.

But Billy first.

She makes a fist around the keys, sticks the F-150 key out between pointer and middle finger, the keys next to it between the next two pairs of fingers. Pathetic, she knows—a practical defense in a parking lot, but not in a forest haunted by a predator with eyes too high to swing at.

She wants to call out to Billy, but that'll only attract the monster. Instead, Christine minds every footstep as she hugs the tree line, leaving Armentia behind. She can't believe the quiet of the forest—nothing moves anywhere, it seems. Her own feet crash and snap through the debris gathered around the base of every tree, so she limps out into road, for the quieter sound of footsteps in the soft snowfall. Wind whispers through the needles and the fine branches above her. Something rustles louder in the distance, and she freezes in place. She squeezes the keys lest they rattle. One of them stabs into the palm of her hand, and she just squeezes harder. She holds her breath but the distant rustle doesn't repeat. She exhales through her teeth and takes a slow step toward the sound, then can't decide exactly which way it came from. Her eyes sweep the trees to that side—if she turns her head the collar of her down jacket drowns out all other sound.

The creature walks toward her. Head down, it bends its neck this way and that to avoid tree trunks. It tilts its head around another trunk, and the whole thing, as big as her car, it vanishes in the muted gray and brown of the forest.

She imagined it—she couldn't believe those hooves, those enormous legs, made no sound.

But it appears again, just a bit closer, and she spins around in the snow, almost losing her balance, squeezing the keys in her fist, as if they'd do any good at all, and runs.

She shoots across the road and sprints through the trees, counting on the thing's antlers to keep it going slow. Christine leans into the run, hopes gravity will pull her forward and her bad ankle won't shoot out from under her. Dodging the trees at this speed, she can't be sure of direction, and just hopes she doesn't head back to that marsh.

When a building appears in the distance she darts to the far side of it, hoping she can put it between her and the thing—though she hasn't turned to see if it's coming, doesn't want to spare even a half a second. The building is bigger than Cabin Eight, the clearing behind it bigger than the space where Haiku died. If she's found the office, she'll get Armentia's truck and drive back to look for Billy, though she's sure the monster could run a truck off the road.

A bright plastic structure like the doghouse stands in the backyard, next to a black box the size of a car. She collapses at the box. A plastic sheet covers it, buttoned in place at the corners. It's a hot tub, covered for winter, and the bright plastic structure is a slide, a child's slide. A barred gate covers sliding glass doors on the back of the building—she's found the deluxe cabin, Armentia's fancy suite.

Something snaps behind her, and she turns. A hot

cloud rises from the nostrils of the creature, too close for her not to have heard it chasing her. The bones of its face move back and forth as the mouth falls open.

Christine shoots past the side of the cabin into the road. Antlers crack against wood behind her. She hooks around to keep the cabin between her and the monster, its black, yawning mouth, and movement catches her eye in a window. For a second she thinks the thing has come through the house, but a person moves inside.

Her son.

Billy stands by a fridge, reflected in the refrigerator door. Hands raised. He looks from one hand to the other. If he sees her he does not look up.

The front door of the house stands open. She lunges at it, but the monster comes around the corner of the house. She could get in the door, close it before the thing reaches her—but she stumbles into the street instead, looks back to make sure the thing comes after her.

She could have imagined the boy in the kitchen. Armentia would not leave the place unlocked. Not the deluxe suite, with its shiny steel fridge. She wouldn't leave the place unlocked any more than Christine would lead the monster to her son.

It ambles after her. She pours on everything she has, ignores the pain, and the thing trots along without making a noise, no noise louder than Christine's gasps— she sucks cold air as fast as she can get it.

In her son's hands, two things. His phone. Always. Something smaller in the other.

She only hopes he found the Wi-Fi password. On the kitchen counter. Next to the coffee pot.

She can distract the creature, can put more distance, as much as she can, between herself and Billy, the monster and her Billy-Goat, as much distance as she can.

She flicks her eyes over her shoulder. Just long enough. The shape is there, chases her, trots after her. Chases her, instead of her son.

The thought of her son figuring out how to get help, it powers her legs when they should stop, it keeps her lungs pumping when they want to collapse.

She follows her own footsteps from earlier. Two sets, coming and going—she adds a third more frantic set of tracks. She had been headed the right way to find the fancy cabin. The deluxe suite.

The mangled Toyota, front end crushed in, sits swamped in snow up the side of the driver's door. The engine shows through the shredded hood.

If she climbed onto the roof of her cabin, could the thing reach her there?

She stumbles over scattered firewood, her boot sliding across the first step, and pain slices through one side of her body. The back of her head connects with one of the pieces of wood she'd dropped. Her good leg slips through the space between the steps and she scrambles backward like a crab, flips herself, banging her head against the car's bumper, then shoots up inside, Armentia's keys still in her fist.

They'd left the cabin's front door open when the thing surprised them in the driveway, and she doesn't think to close it now.

They must have left the freezer door open. Frost fills the entire space, fills the corners, hangs from the beams overhead. She makes deep impressions as she steps into Cabin Eight.

She tosses the keys onto the table by the sofa. Armentia's keys slide past Christine's own car keys, disappear off the back of the skinny table.

Christine is surprised to see her keys covered in frost. She'd told Billy to grab them. Saw Billy grab them instead of the hatchet.

He grabbed the wrong keys. The keys Armentia had given her at check-in.

That's how he got into the deluxe cabin. Otherwise he'd still be running through the woods, wouldn't he?

And the monster would be with him.

Instead of here. With her.

It steps through the doorway.

Good. This is what she wants.

Its antlers clear away the icicles hanging from the doorjamb. Snow muffles the rapping of the hooves on the floorboards.

The creature speaks. That voice. It says her name again: "Christine." The same voice. It asks her why she thinks it's here.

Christine backs toward to the cold black fireplace. "Because I can see you." She kicks the hatchet, but doesn't reach for it. The pain in her leg is nothing, but her hand aches where she's squeezed the keys so hard. A little hatchet-shaped snow angel drags across the floor.

The front hooves lift up from the floor. Fists open and it flexes its fingers, shakes them loose, as it rises on its hind legs. "Why would I come?" it asks. The bones that encircle the head, they crash through the ice above, smash the last lightbulb, rain ice and glass down on Christine.

She says she knows she screwed up. She says Derek's name, says her husband's name.

The creature bends its huge head down and shakes it. The bones of the face shift and pull, and the antlers clack against the rafters. Eyes roll loose inside the sockets beneath the bony ridge of the brow.

"I grant what souls desire," it says. The back legs stay bent under the massive torso—if the thing stood at its full height it might go on forever. "Their wishes."

Christine asks it, "Whose?"

"There is no one else here." The creature reaches behind it, and pulls the door shut, scraping away the ice that had gathered in the threshold.

# ACKNOWLEDGEMENTS

Thank you, first and foremost, to Christopher Brooks, without whom this book would certainly not exist, and with whom everything I write becomes so much more horrifying and wonderful.

Thank you to George Sandison, Daniel Carpenter, Elora Hartway, and the entire team at Titan Books, who welcomed this sinister seasonal chiller into the fold and championed it every step of the way.

Thank you to my beloved agent Italia Gandolfo, who puts up with me on my best days and my worst.

Thank you to Jamie Flanagan, to Chuck Palahniuk, and to Stephanie Wytovich—for everything.

Lastly, thank you to Camp Rotary and to that one horrid solstice spent deep in the Pennsylvania Wilds where everything that could go wrong, did. This one's for you.

# ABOUT THE AUTHOR

**Lindy Ryan** is a Bram Stoker Award® Nominee and a Silver Falchion Award-winning editor, author, professor, short-film director, and anthologist whose books have received starred reviews from *Publishers Weekly, Booklist,* and *Library Journal.* A *Publishers Weekly* Star Watch Honoree, Ryan is the author of *Bless Your Heart, Cold Snap,* and more. She is the current author-in-residence at *Rue Morgue,* the world's leading horror culture and entertainment brand, and the "Chill Quill" columnist at BookTrib. Her guest articles and features include *NPR, BBC Culture, Irish Times, Daily Mail,* and more. In 2022, Ryan was named one of horror's most masterful anthology curators, and she has been declared a "champion for women's voices in horror" by *Shelf Awareness* (2023). Her animated short film, "Trick or Treat, Alistair Gray", based on her children's book of the same name, won the Grand Prix Award at the 2022 ANMTN Awards. Lindy also writes contemporary romance that has been adapted for film. On social @ LindyRyanWrites and at LindyRyanWrites.com.

For more fantastic fiction, author events,
exclusive excerpts, competitions, limited editions and more

VISIT OUR WEBSITE
**titanbooks.com**

LIKE US ON FACEBOOK
**facebook.com/titanbooks**

FOLLOW US ON TWITTER AND INSTAGRAM
**@TitanBooks**

EMAIL US
**readerfeedback@titanemail.com**